8op

Murder at the Bull Hotel

GW00601936

Printed in Great Bri

Published by Abbeyhill Publishing Ltd.
Abbeyhill, Broadway, Letchworth UK

⊰⊱ *CHAPTER 1* ⊰⊱

It was Thursday.

I was walking along Bancroft in the old Hertfordshire market town of Hitchin, hurrying along would be more precise for I was late, and I hated to be late but I had been talking to an old friend, who had her share of problems and wanted to share them with me. I was a good listener and had felt torn between being too abrupt with my friend who was distressed, and running behind schedule for an appointment at my hotel, the Bull. It was two years since my parents had died, unhappily within a few months of each other. They had always been exceedingly close, had spent their lives doing everything together, when my father died I know my mother had, naturally, missed him dreadfully. They had been the proprietors of a small, very old hotel in Hitchin and this, at the age of 24 years, I had inherited. At present I was trying to improve not only its already fairly high standards, but also its fairly meagre profitability. I found the task daunting.

On this particular Thursday morning I had arranged to meet a young couple who were, I hoped, to book their wedding reception at the Bull but I was late for the appointment and the weather was very warm indeed. Rushing about did nothing to improve my complexion and I was getting hot and sticky. On leaving Rosemary, my friend, who I fear, was not much comforted by our conversation, I made my way through a throng of people along the churchyard shopping area, across the old market place. I slipped down Bucklesbury and into Tilehouse Street where the hotel had stood for so many centuries. I entered the hotel and looked around, the reception area was empty, coolish, tidy and welcoming. Gloria, my secretary, girl Friday and Gofer, was on the telephone but mouthed to me that I would have time for a shower.

'Does it show that much?' I asked.

Gloria nodded. 'One of the problems of being fair.'

'That's not fair.'

The hotel, which had borne the name of the Bull, for several hundred years, was a hotch potch of corridors, rooms off, staircases and corners. It had grown over the centuries absorbing neighbouring properties and having extensions built on. An intriguing rambling building friendly, old and well used but one not easy to modernise. The public rooms themselves, the lobby, reception dining room, function room and lounge were quite classy, although I was not at all happy with the saloon bar. A few of the bedrooms had been completely refurbished, I was quite proud of them but by no means had all of them received new furnishings, yet they were bright and cheerful. Even my own room way up in the attic was decorated with what I believed to be considerable taste, but the decoration could not camouflage the cracks in the walls, the sloping timbers, the creaking floor, and on such a day as this, it was hot, like an oven. I stripped, discarding my preferred short skirt and T-shirt, showered and reappearing down the stairs. I walked back to the reception area not too long after my clients had arrived, dressed in a long black skirt and formal white blouse, a black jacket and sensible shoes. I had changed from fun loving to business woman.

In reception Gloria and Ian, a work experience lad just coming to the end of his first week at the hotel, were in deep discussion. I raised an inquisitive eyebrow as I passed.

'It is not a great problem,' explained Gloria. 'We had two guests checked in almost together, and Ian inadvertently gave the keys to Room 16 to a Mr Jeffery Barrett, although he was meant to have Room 26, and he gave the keys to Room 26 to a Mr Richard Jenkins who was meant to have Room 16. Neither of the guests know of the mix up and both seem happy with their rooms which are very similar. I was just helping Ian to sort out the computer records.

'I really am most sorry,' said Ian looking embarrassed. No doubt he would learn, perhaps a little more supervision was needed; I made a mental note to make sure that it was available to him. Ian was a really pleasant person and would succeed but it was taking just a little longer than one would have expected for him to learn the ropes. All other aspects of his work, punctuality, dress, attitude, enthusiasm were first class and both the guests and the other staff got on well with him. I had hopes that he might go far but perhaps slowly.

'Your clients are waiting' said Gloria, as usual on the ball she nodded towards the sitting room where a couple were talking in low tones. I walked to greet my guests clutching a copy of our brochure and tariff and put on what I hoped was a welcoming but business-like smile and apologised for being late. I introduced myself as Lucy White, that being my name, and the meeting began. They were what I would call a chunky couple both rather over weight but standing close to each other, obviously deeply in love. The hotel was blessed with a very old ballroom which provided one of the best function rooms in town, it was there that many a wedding feast had taken place. In olden days auctions were held there, sometimes town meetings, it was the town's first cinema, and once or twice, long ago, was the place where the Chief Magistrate held his court. Recently we hosted wedding receptions several times a month, they proved to be a great success. My meeting with the couple continued, we were usually successful selling the hotel, as it was delightfully old, the prices were reasonable and the service we gave was better than most.

'And does the cost include the table decorations?' asked the young lady.

'Yes, we provide fresh flowers for each table but if you want anything special, you must provide it yourselves.'

'Will ours be the only function that weekend? asked the young man, the first time he had spoken. 'I only ask because at the last wedding reception I went to, the reception was in one room and a funeral wake in another adjoining room. Mind you, they seemed to be having much more fun at the wake.'

'I promise, yours will be the only function on that day.'

'Mind you,' the man went on, 'when the bride's father called the groom by the bride's previous boyfriend's name it caused a real rumpus.'

'It's easy for the father to get these details wrong,' I said.

The questions then came one after the other, all from the lady. I had answered these same questions numerous times before and indeed all were in the brochure clutched in the lady's hand but that is par for the course.

'A real rumpus,' the man added.

Meanwhile hotel life sprung into its routine, teas were served to a group of blue rinse ladies who often chose Thursdays to meet informally in the hotel lounge; guests continued to be booked in, asking Ian or Gloria about parking, room service, keys, meal times; some staff came on duty, mainly the restaurant and bar staff, some staff went off duty, mainly the chambermaids and cleaners. All quite normal with nothing to foretell the extraordinary sequence of events which were about to unfurl.

That evening the Bull Hotel was hosting a dinner dance for a local fundraising charity, a branch of the NSPCC. On such an occasion the staff were stretched but we still made sure that the ordinary diners were not ignored in the dining room which would, I suspect, be about three quarters full. Altogether twelve people were staying overnight in the hotel, including Jeffrey Barrett and Richard Jenkins. To please my bank manager it would have been nice to have just a few more bookings, perhaps I should rethink the advertising.

Richard Jenkins was a boisterous man almost larger than life, a local man of whom I had heard but never formally met, save to serve him in the bar. I was a little surprised as to why he should choose to stay at the hotel at all, rather than spend the night at home in so far as I was aware he only lived a mile or two outside Hitchin, off in the Ickleford direction; however that was his business. It did seem a little strange, perhaps his family were away. I did not know and it was really no concern of mine but that did not stop me being nosy. I gathered he was very rich.

Of Jeffrey Barrett I knew a little more. We had chatted on previous occasions when he had stayed at the hotel, indeed he was almost a regular, Hitchin being his base town but chose not to live what would have been a lonely life in a house or flat. Rather he much preferred hotel life, meals cooked for him, beds made, laundry done and a friendly bar. No question of having to drink and drive; it meant having to live out of a suitcase but years ago, he had, he told me, found a way of making even that acceptable. Jeffrey Barrett kept four sets of clothes, renewing them frequently, but never varying. He had two identical suits, shirts and ties for business and two identical casual shirts, jumpers and trousers in which he relaxed. I gathered he was not a poor man, far from it, it was just that he had no interest in clothes, as long as they were clean and he did not look out of place. To him, it mattered not a jot what he wore. His passion was military history, especially C19 military history.

Years ago, he had bought a fully serviced flat in Hitchin, but had never lived there. The flat was a shrine to war; books, medals, models and memorabilia of battles. Every room had a different war theme, a private collection of some value which he liked to think of as his museum. One day, he promised himself, he would show it off to the public, but not just yet. To many, it would have seemed a strange life, yet it suited him. He had no ties, no money worries, he was content or so he said.

The day wore on into its well-adjusted routine; soon after 7 o'clock the first of the people attending the charity dinner, the relievers as Ian called them, arrived for the function, all already in high spirits. The band which had been setting itself up during most of the afternoon was now playing. Just what it was playing was not immediately obvious to me, probably a work composed by one of its members to save paying royalties, that is what they usually did, saving the best numbers, those known to all, until later. The music they were playing was jolly enough. By 7.30 I was delighted to see that the hotel bars, the dining room, and the function room were all packed. The charity dinner was a sit down meal starting at 8 'clock, meanwhile men queued at the bar, and ladies chatted in the Ladies and the music changed to tunes which were more easily recognisable; the staff who were on duty really earned their keep, the hotel was buzzing, it was grand.

I walked to the kitchens just to check things. The starter for the charity dinner of summer tomato and basil galette was fully prepared. The lemon syllabubs were resting in the fridge, roast racks of lamb waiting to be roasted with a rosemary, Dijon and garlic sauce was causing Claude my French chef some anguish, the lamb must be pink, just right. He was a professional with a short fuse, so I had to tread warily, making sure that he thought I was calling in to compliment him, rather than to inspect or criticise him.

Jeffrey Barrett bumped into me catching me between my tour of the kitchens and the lounge, we had a short natter. He was not going to the charity dinner, rather he dined alone save for the company of a bottle of claret but he said he was quite used to that, and enjoyed people watching. Leaving him I wandered from bars to dining room to function room to make sure wrinkles were smoothed out before they became obstacles. Often I would have preferred to stay in one place but I was a figurehead on these evenings and needed to be seen. I returned to the saloon bar crossed to the public bar and there, saw Jeffrey Barrett again. By this time he had drunk quite a bit. He had the somewhat strange habit of ordering the same drink

8

as the person to whom he was talking. This was not quite as alarming as it may sound, as he was only talking to men of about his own age, in a public bar, everyone there was drinking beer, whisky or lager. At one time I had thought of closing the public bar and enlarging the saloon bar to increase profits a little but my father had always loved the atmosphere in there. More earthy he would say, I am not sure that it was, except perhaps the language which probably changed when the men there saw me. The public bar was thought to be a male preserve. My accountant was always telling me never to be sentimental, that if it would make more money the public bar should be closed but somehow it was not that easy.

Walking back to the function room I passed through reception. Ian was still on duty, he seemed edgy, perhaps he was just tired, I went over to talk with him for a little while. By this time the meals had been eaten, people were dancing, talking, drinking. One lady lost her handbag, she must have complained to the whole hotel and insisted on calling in the police. Indeed she came into reception to do so, she was very cross until Ian told her that someone had already handed the bag in to him, they had found the handbag where the lady had left it in the Ladies lavatory. A couple of men had a bit too much to drink so I eased them into a taxi to take them home, a light bulb broke in the men's loo, I added it to the maintenance schedule.

The evening wore on. The NSPCC dinner ended,

people streamed home. Evidently it had raised a little more than the sum expected so the organisers were very happy, the bars closed, I watched as the hotel slowly sunk into its night-time garb, one after another the staff went off duty saying goodnight to me. One after another the guests went up to their rooms, no doubt undressed, got into bed. Some showering first, some forgetting to. Everything grew quiet. It was time I went to bed too.

Friday morning started early for me. I was the proprietor of the hotel, but I was also attending college, studying for a Masters Degree in English History; I was far from certain what I wanted to do with my life but I was sure that I didn't want to spend all of it managing a small hotel in Hitchin. Realising this, some time ago I had appointed Martin Lynch as my manager to look after the day-to-day running of the hotel whilst I retained the responsibilities for the cash flow, hiring staff, and premises. Many things we did on a joint basis, advertising was one of these. Martin had taken three weeks holiday to tour his beloved France, he was due to return to work the following Monday when I was due back at college, until then my responsibilities and duties seemed endless but I had done it all many times before. I used to make sure that I was always the last one about at night and that I locked up, but that soon proved impossible. I became much too tired. I was anxious to get in some exercise at some point during the day as it helped me cope with the pressures, so an early start was called for, Fridays were usually busy.

Tripping down the staircase at around 7 o'clock I checked that the debris from the previous night had already been cleared away, the Hoovers were busy, sun streamed through the open doors and windows letting out the fuggy air from last night. Weather wise it was going to be another glorious day with temperatures rising to the high eighties. Early risers were breakfasting, paying their dues at reception and relinquishing their keys before leaving, their rooms would soon be attacked and sanitised by my staff and made ready for the next guests. The guests booking in for the weekend were a very different bunch from those booking mid week, they were mainly business clientele. At weekends it was usually families and couples, especially when a wedding reception was to be held. Friendly bustle rippled through the hotel, at least I think it was friendly, no doubt there were undercurrents of which I was not aware. Most managers think they know everything that is going on around them but few of them do. Between the staff there would be bossiness, dislike, rivalry, admiration, no doubt sexual attraction too, such was human nature. I walked around the building helping at one point, authorising something at another, and taking stock at a third. I had been brought up to hotel life and had lived at the hotel for the whole of my 26 years, I think I knew the ins and outs of every job, having done most of them for my parents at one time or another I am pleased to say that the hotel experienced very few genuine complaints from guests. I hate dealing with irate ladies, all one can really do is to stand and take it.

A system had been worked out whereby the chambermaids, and there were six of them, were informed by whoever was on reception as soon as a guest had paid and checked out. Then with their trolleys in tow, the chambermaids replaced, dusted and scrubbed one bedroom after another. This they did on that Friday morning, and by noon, there were only two rooms left to be done, those occupied by Jeffrey Barrett in Room 16 and Richard Jenkins in Room 26. Checkout time was officially 11 o'clock but latitude was given, especially for clients who were staying for a day or two. It was past 11.30 before I was approached by one of the chambermaids to see if Room 16 and Room 26 might be knocked up. They never liked to do this themselves as sometimes they came across a male guest without clothes on, whether he was found naked accidentally or deliberately there was no means of telling. Most of the chambermaids were middle aged, and married with children. Just why they thought I was best suited to handle this situation was never made clear; but to them it was the manager's job. I was the manager so it was up to me. I tapped on the door of room 16, but received no reply. I tapped again then let myself into the room with my pass key. The curtains were still drawn and it was gloomy in the room, especially after the bright sunlit corridors. My eyes had to adjust. I coughed 'Excuse me Sir but it is after 11.30, and you are checkng out today.'

The man yawned. 'It can't be so late,' said a voice from the bed. 'Heavens I must get up, I am so sorry, I have over slept. Can you give me half an hour or so and you can be rid of me?'

'There is no real hurry Sir,' I said. 'Shall I arrange for some breakfast to be brought up to you in your room?'

'That would by very kind, thank you just toast and coffee would be splendid, oh yes and if I could have a bit of jam and a boiled egg or two.'

I smiled and turned to go, left the room, and asked Yvonne, my senior chambermaid as a favour to me, to bring a tray with toast and coffee and a boiled egg or two up to Room 16. She said that she would.

'And what about Room 26, he is still asleep but he is staying over the weekend,' said Susan one of the other chambermaids.

'Oh let's leave him be for a bit. If he really wants a lie in, so be it,' I said. 'Do his room immediately after lunch would you, we must try to keep guests happy. He will probably wake up in a moment or two anyway.'

Yvonne was not the happiest of my staff, a little on the surly side but without too much of an objection she directed those under her to various tasks and she herself went off to organise the late breakfast for Room 16. I went to reception to get Mr Jenkins' bill made out and then continued my tour of the hotel.

Just after lunch there is a quiet period in most hotels, the Bull was no exception. Guests are snoozing, shopping or have yet to check in. The public rooms are quiet, little if any food is being prepared, the cleaning is largely finished. Often I used this quiet period to take some exercise and today I had organised to ride my friend's horse; I had ridden ponies and horses most of my life, having had a pony as a child, later entering gymkhana and even cross country events with the Pony Club. Those days were gone, but the tiny hamlet of Todds Green just by the village of St Ippolytts a minute or two outside Hitchin, stabled my friends thoroughbred, 'Archie'. In his youth Archie had been a racehorse of world renown, after he had retired, she had bought him and even in retirement Archie gave an exciting ride: given a clear track ahead he galloped wonderfully.

So it was that I slipped out of the hotel once the lunch time crush had eased, and drove down Tilehouse Street, up to the Three Moorhens Roundabout, and then into and through St Ippolytts. The stable yard was usually very quiet at that time of day, with only the horse I was going to ride, Archie, looking out of the top part of the doorway, the other horses were usually grazing in the three large paddocks surrounding the stables or out being ridden, but today things were different.

The stables housed three horses, Toby, Archie and

McTell, and two ponies Crackers and Ceaser. Crackers was now very old indeed, a tiny pony of 12 hands on whom all of the local children had been taught to ride and now was really just a pet. All of the horses were in their stables that afternoon their long necks stretched over their stable doors as the equine dentist Charles Duggan was paying his six monthly visit. It was the first time I had met him and we started chatting immediately. I don't think I am one to take an instant liking or disliking to anyone but I did find myself warming to Charles. He seemed happy, carefree and very few people I meet are carefree. Most of my friends seem to be worried, sometimes about money, sometimes over lack of boyfriends or how to get rid of a boyfriend. Many say that they have to work too hard, some are jealous or concerned about one or other of the hundreds of problems that beset us all. Charles seemed genuinely happy in his work, contented and as I said, carefree. He was in his mid twenties, sun burnt or perhaps it was wind burnt and was mighty strong but appeared caring as well, especially regarding the horses under his charge. I loved his voice, what is it that attracts to one voice but not another? It wasn't long before I realised that Charles was rather nice; he compared well with most of the men I knew, at least, on first sighting he did. By the time I drove up, Charles had already seen to Crackers, Ceaser and McTell.

'If you are going to ride him, shall I do Archie next?' Charles asked, picking up a gruesome instrument, a set of steel jaws laced with leather straps.

'Yes thanks, but you are not going to use that on Archie are you?' I said fearfully.

'That's what we use, would you help? Get Archie out of the stable please.'

I picked up the head collar, gave Archie a stroke or two on the forelock, put on his head collar and led him out into the yard.

'Hold him steady please', and with that Charles inserted the huge steel jaws into Archie's mouth, wound the leather around his head and secured it with a buckle. By making adjustments, Archie's mouth was kept wide open, ready for a file, about two feet long to be inserted. Each tooth was given a few minutes attention with this mammoth rasp.

I was becoming more and more uneasy. 'You'll hurt him, he will rear.'

'No I won't. I wouldn't hurt you old fellow would I? He will feel much happier when I have finished.'

And sure enough Archie just stood whilst his teeth were filed, leaving me to ponder on the equine dentist himself, Charles had strong arms, brown curly hair, big brown eyes, an easy manner, and a way with horses and people.

'Tell me about your work?' I asked him.

'I have the best job in the world,' said Charles. 'I really love it, I like being with horses, I like making life more comfortable for them, I enjoy chatting to their owners. It is similar to a human dentist's job in a way, but without the patient being able to tell you what is wrong. We check off each tooth, sometimes extract, usually just grind down, rinse and check again. With horses' teeth, they tend to get very sharp which can cause them a lot of pain. Grinding down the sharp edge of the tooth makes it much more comfortable for the horse.'

'What do you mean rinse, how do you rinse out a horses mouth?'

'In the bucket there is a rinse solution, very similar to the solution you have at your dentist. I use a large syringe, that one over there. I take an amount up, and squirt it into the horse's mouth. If that isn't done, little bits of ground tooth would be left around his tongue.'

Caroline who owned the stable yard, came up to talk to us. 'Hello Lucy, you look a picture of health. Why don't you both go for a ride, the horses need exercising?' she said. 'You could ride McTell if you would like to Charles. I would come with you but I must deliver my children to a party; anyway I am sure you can manage very well indeed without me.'

'It's very tempting, what do you say?' asked Charles.

'Good idea, if you have time. I thought you were working.' I said,

'It's Friday afternoon, Toby won't mind waiting a little, this is my last call today, let's go.' So we did. We groomed both horses carefully, checked hooves for stones, selected bridle and saddle, sorted out the martingales, did up girths and mounted the horses using the old oak mounting block. We set off walking the horses up the track which formed part of the Hertfordshire Way, it was hundreds and hundreds of years old, coming from pre history. On our left, five ponies grazed in a four acre paddock, on our right a large field set aside under the EU farm policy. We walked our horses on passed an oak tree which looked old but I do not know whether it was, and several holly bushes sprouting from the mechanically trimmed hedge. Reaching the top of an incline the hedges dropped away and on the right a wide vista opened up. The ground ran down to the Codicote Hitchin road about two miles away, and then climbed to the horizon, undulating farm land, trees and farm houses, criss crossed with bridle paths. Quite delightful. The view on the right was not quite so picturesque, being of the top five storeys of the local Lister Hospital peeping through the landscape. We broke into a trot along this path, down through a dell, joined another track and cantered, an easy canter for about half a mile before pulling up to a walk again. We didn't want to get the horses too hot.

'Tell me something about yourself,' said Charles.

'Me!' I said, thinking immediately that it was one of the most stupid things I could have said.

'I was born in Hitchin and went to the local Girls School, then to Nottingham University. My family have always owned the Bull Hotel and I have always lived there. I used to have to help them, doing everything from washing up to making beds to running the reception. I used to be 'The Boots'. Guests would leave their shoes outside their doors each night, and I would have to collect them all up, clean and polish them, and return them to the correct door before they woke, if the shoes ever got muddled up, I was in for it'.

'You mean they walloped you.'

'No, but the guests would have a go at me. Not surprising, it must have been very annoying for them to have returned outside their room door in the morning, just one of their own shoes, and one of somebody else's. Some evenings I would clean 15 or 16 pairs of shoes or boots, hard work for a ten year old. I did not really mind except when friends went off enjoying themselves, asked me to join them but I found myself stuck making beds. My parents used to work very hard, it is not an easy task running an hotel.'

'And now it is all yours,' said Charles.

'Yes, I inherited the place two years ago, I have no brothers or sisters so am on my own apart from an aunt and uncle, auntie Iris and uncle George. They live in a small village in Dorset. They really are super people but I seldom see them. My uncle used to be an inspector in the local police force but they retired and moved away from Hitchin. They spend much of their time in France nowadays. I feel lonely sometimes, a bit burdened by the hotel, on the other hand it can be really good. I read somewhere about a son who had inherited an historic home.

It was a wonderful place, with a deer park, and heirlooms everywhere. Everyone envied him, but he found it a terrible responsibility, and sometimes would have preferred to sell up and be normal, what he called normal. I know the feeling which is why I started a masters degree course, it is something completely different.'

'A masters degree?'

'Yes, at Colchester University, History. I am writing a thesis on how the Conquest changed life in England, and how the effects have rippled down the centuries. Did you know that in Bedfordshire, about 15 miles away there is a park called Wrest Park, where the de Grey family lived from the Conquest down to 1917? History is fascinating.'

There was a silence between us, I think I must have gone on a bit too long. 'Tell me about you,' I said.

'I was born in Bury, just north of Manchester, but moved to Hackney when I was a toddler. My parents were not very rich, but very close and we spent a lot of time together. I wanted to be a vet but couldn't get the right grades in my exams. I thought of becoming a farrier, then found out about being an equine dentist and never looked back.'

'Are you married?' I actually wanted to know if he had a girlfriend, but wasn't going to ask.

'No, not yet.'

Now what did that mean. We rode on for a while, and then back towards the stables squeezing past a line of six riders lead by Vi, Caroline's neighbour and one of the best and most experienced of horsewomen.

'I do have a sort of part-time job as well as being a dentist,' said Charles.

'Tell me.'

'I horse sit.'

'Horse sit?'

'Yes, a bit like people who house sit and look after plants and dogs. When people are away or unwell, I visit their horses, usually twice a day. In the winter I rug them, muck them out, feed, groom and check them over. If the vet, or farrier is needed, I can contact them.'

'And in the summer?'

'In the summer, I still visit them twice a day, often the horses are left out, but if it is too hot or wet I bring them in. It's not an arduous task, and there are long periods, especially in the spring and summer, when I don't horse sit at all. Summer holidays and skiing times are the busiest.'

We rode on for a while in single file so conversation stopped until we were back in the yard, but it was an easy silence. We said our goodbyes, I thanked him for his company and left, I wondered if we would meet again. Caroline had driven off somewhere in our absence; otherwise we might have shared a pot of tea.

After riding I always felt relaxed, happy and fulfilled. 'Much better than sex.' I said to myself as I made my way back to Hitchin and the hotel, but I did wonder what Charles would be like in bed. Driving back to the Bull, I was thoughtful. I knew I would have a hectic Friday evening in front of me, it was always so on Fridays especially when a function was being hosted at the hotel, and indeed so it proved but even worse than I could possibly imagine. As soon as I drove into the hotel yard I saw the police car parked where nobody else would dare to park, it was parked on double yellow lines under the very nose of the local traffic warden. Police usually meant trouble with a licensing problem, but I wasn't aware that we had had any difficulties.

I walked into the hotel, and found a flustered Ian behind the reception desk.

'Hello Ian, what's happening?' I asked him. 'Why are the police outside the hotel?'

'Big problems, Mr Jenkins, in Room 26, he was found dead in his room, they say that he may have been poisoned.'

❧ CHAPTER 2 ❧

'Ian, calm down,' I said. 'Now, please say again.'

'Mr Jenkins, who was staying in Room 26 last night, he was found dead by Yvonne when she went in to do the room. She had a terrible time for at first she thought he was just asleep, and she tried to wake him by shaking his shoulder. She has had to go home but she did call an ambulance, and the ambulance men called the police and the police came. As you see, they are still there.'

'Well Mr Jenkins has probably had a heart attack. It is very sad, but none of us knew him, and people do have heart attacks and unhappily sometimes they die of them.'

'You may be right, but the ambulance man said Mr Jenkins, except that he did not call him Mr Jenkins, may have been poisoned. The man said that it didn't look like a heart attack to him, and he says he sees several people suffering from heart attacks every week. He doesn't see so many cases of poisoning but he thinks that Mr Jenkins may have been poisoned. Anyway the police want to speak to you urgently, I've been told to ask you to go up straight away?'

Still wearing my jodhpurs, and no doubt smelling a bit of horses, I went up to Room 26, and introduced myself to the two uniformed policeman who were walking up and down presumably on guard duty.

'Now Miss,' said one police constable after I had

introduced myself, 'we have an unexplained death here so nothing must be touched until things are sorted out. We are instructed to stay here at least for the moment, there will be several other people coming and we should be grateful if you would arrange to show them all up.'

'Of course I will,' said I, 'in the meantime would you like a cup of tea and a sandwich?'

'Thank you, but not until we can come downstairs. Best not to have any other beverages in here, it might confuse things.'

'Do you know how he died?'

'Don't rightly know Miss.'

'I will leave you to it then.'

It was going to be difficult, nobody ever likes death in an hotel, well nobody ever likes death near them at all. I slipped upstairs to my room to change into formal business wear, I drew a deep breath went downstairs, no doubt still smelling of horses and entered the reception lobby, where I found the staff in a huddle: I asked them to get on with their jobs went to the kitchen and talked to the chef, went to the bars to help out the staff there. Everyone seemed to work with a little more energy when I was about, but this might have been an illusion, perhaps I was getting power crazy. Usually I enjoyed the crush of happy people in the hotel drinking or dining; the staff working hard and as a team, the building itself being used to the full. I found myself a bit frightened, as if I realised I could not quite cope with everything. My confidence had drained away, yet with my highly trained team, I didn't really have much to do, thankfully it all carried on as it should.

It's dreadful if I have a big worry, it dominates my mind. I try to distract myself by thinking of other things, and this succeeds for a while but then all the horrible thoughts float to the surface again. I could not help thinking that this was all very bad for the hotel.

The afternoon and evening wore slowly on, everyone seemed in good spirits; the end of the week, celebrating that it was Friday. I was just checking the lounge with thoughts of returning to the bars after about half an hour when one of the police constables came up to me. He had obviously been searching for me and was quite relieved when our paths crossed.

'Detective Chief Inspector Blake has been put in charge of the case Miss, he is here now and he wants to talk to you.'

'Where is he?'

'Still in Room 26, hurry along there if you would please Miss, he is not a man who likes to be kept waiting.' Nodding I made my way there, took a deep breath, tapped on the closed door, and waited for it to be opened by the second police constable.

'I gather I am wanted,' I said.

'Yes, come on in Miss please,' The room was full of people all of them doing things, photographing, men with notebooks, someone who seemed to be collecting finger prints. A middle aged man stopped what he was doing and walked up to me. 'I am Detective Chief Inspector Blake Miss,' he said looking around him. 'This room is getting too full of people, is there somewhere else we can talk?'

I led the Inspector to the manager's office, we sat down and I studied his face. He must have been about 45 years old, he was very serious, a little on the fat side but his voice was confident and authoritarian.

'I regret to tell you that the person who occupied Room 26 in your hotel last night has died. The exact cause of death isn't yet known but the paramedic thought he was poisoned, so until I have a doctors report I am treating the death as one of poison. I have no idea whether the poisoning was accidental or deliberate, so have an open mind. At present I am just obtaining information, what can you tell me please?'

'Very little,' I said. 'I don't remember meeting Mr Jenkins, although I knew of him by general repute. His name has been in the newspapers, he may have visited the hotel previously, I can easily check, it will be on the computer. I thought Mr Jenkins lived locally and so I was a little surprised that he was staying for the weekend at the Bull, but no doubt he had his reasons for doing so, perhaps his wife is away. I am sorry but I did not check him in, and had nothing to do with him during his stay, I don't think I even saw him.'

'Naturally we are checking with his family and trying to trace who he met last night. If it was poison, could it have come from the hotel fare?' asked D. C. I. Blake.

'Heavens I hope not. I don't know what he ate last night but nobody else has complained of being unwell. Do you really think the poison came from the hotel, that would be dreadful.'

Perhaps not surprisingly D.C.I. Blake ignored my question, he asked me another.

'Did you know him at all personally?'

'I don't think I have ever even met him.'

'Run me through if you would please, what you think would have happened here yesterday. Perhaps from the time Richard Jenkins checked in with your staff at the reception desk downstairs, to the time you retired for the night, so that I can get some idea of the likely sequence of events.'

I outlined the hotel registration procedure, which, heavens above, was ordinary enough; that the guests would present themselves at reception; we would enter their names, addresses and car numbers on a form for the computer, the room key would be handed to them and we would offer to deliver their cases up to the room. I described to the Inspector the hotel lounge, two hotel bars, he said he knew them all, described to the Inspector the restaurant, he said he knew the restaurant. When I had finished speaking he looked at me very thoughtfully. There was quite a long silence and then he said that that was all for now.

Thankfully I was dismissed, and went about my duties. I was very busy for the rest of the day not least because we had a blocked drain in the Ladies lavatory; not easy to sort out really urgently at that time of day, it took ages to persuade someone to come out at very short notice. Lavatories always have top priority in the hotel agenda, there is nothing worse for the bars, the dining room or the bedrooms for an evil smell to prevail. Ladies' lavatories block up three or four times more often than do the Gents. Perhaps it's inevitable. It was not until well past 11 o'clock that evening that I found a moment to myself; shutting myself away in the manager's office, hiding actually the horror of the death made me jittery, however much of a brave face I put on it for the likes of Ian. I was stunned, and was dismayed to hear a knock on the door after only a few minutes of my solitude. I wanted to run away and hide my head in the sand.

'Who is it?' I said very reluctantly. A face appeared, it was Charles.

'Oh it's you.'

'Not much of a greeting.'

'Well, no, sorry. Apart from the riding it has really been a terrible day. Have you heard about Mr Jenkins dying in Room 26, the police think he was poisoned here in my hotel. The room is still sealed off, thank goodness he booked for the whole weekend otherwise I would have guests without a room. Everyone is making funnies about it ... saying "what's your poison" when ordering drinks, or "goodnight I hope I'll see you in the morning, but it may be unlikely" and "my doctor gave me these tablets, I take one in the evening and one if I wake up in the morning" great fun!'

'You sound very gloomy. I can see you really don't want visitors,' said Charles.

'That's very true,' said I, 'but I am not sure I class you as a visitor.'

'Do I stay or go?'

'Stay for a little while, come on in, have a drink?'

'No I am driving, better not drink, thank you,' said Charles. 'My you are tense, sit down for a moment, have you had a drink?'

I explained that I never drank whilst managing the hotel, off the premises it was different.

Charles sat me down on one of the upright chairs, he went behind me. I was too tired to notice really. He started to massage my shoulders, it was a bit annoying at first, I was wearing a blouse with a formal collar, and a dark suit with padded jacket. All he was doing was rubbing cloth against cloth, still if that's what he wanted to do. I suddenly realised that that was probably how he treated his horses. He started to stroke the nape of my neck with finger tip caresses. It tickled at first, then suddenly it was very pleasant indeed. I didn't want him to stop. I could feel a change in my mood.

After a moment or two he eased off my jacket and stroked, pummelled and fingered my taut shoulders. Five minutes later I was a different person, I turned, rose and hugged him. He put his arms around me, traced the outline of my spine from my neck down to the swell of my bottom, and back, again and again. Then he kissed me, stroking my hair.

'You have such wonderful eyes,' he said.

As he kissed me his hand moved lower and lower so that soon his fingers traced the outline of my bottom, he stroked one cheek, then the other and still kissing me, pulled my bottom against him with both hands. I could feel my breasts small as they are, pushing against his chest and was aware of his desire for me.

'Heavens,' I thought, 'can this be happening. I think I want to take it rather more slowly than Charles seems to want to do.'

Very gently I broke away. 'I think it's time you were going home, but I am glad you came.' I added as I didn't want to close the door on what might be the start of something promising. 'I can see tomorrow I'll need to have my wits about me, it is going to be a really difficult day.'

And it was.

Even before breakfast D.C.I. Blake called on me

accompanied by a very attractive police constable. I wonder if such an attractive young lady is relevant to his job, they led me into Room 26. I was pleased to see that there was now no trace of the poor man, I suppose people get used to being around dead bodies but I never have.

'Do you know why the deceased was staying at your hotel,' asked D.C.I. Blake as his opening gambit.

'I suppose because it is a really good hotel,' I replied a bit glibly really.

'No doubt it is, but evidently the real reason he was staying here was because he wanted to take you over.'

'Take me over! Take me over what?'

'No, no, I mean, he was going to try to buy the hotel from you at a knock down price, or that's what the papers in his pocket seem to infer.'

'But it is not for sale, I would never sell it.'

'Well it is a puzzle, we do need please your full co-operation.'

'You have it,' I said aghast, 'but I don't know anything that will help you, as far as I know I never even met the man. I certainly did not serve him poison.'

'Let us start from the beginning. How did he book the room?'

'I will have to check, but I expect it was by telephone. Most people seem to look up hotels on the Internet, but prefer to actually book, by talking to someone. Very few guests do it all by post.'

'I will need to know and who actually checked him in.'

'It would have been Ian Witty, our work experience lad, he has only been with us a week.'

'When, at what time did he check in?'

'It would have been at about 2.45 pm on Thursday but you had better ask Ian direct, I was not in reception at the time.'

'I must try to ascertain the deceased's movements during the whole of the evening. Are you certain he didn't approach you?'

'Fairly certain, if you had a photograph of him it would help. I saw so many people last night that I had never seen before. I think you must be wrong, he could not have wanted to buy the Bull, anyway no proposal or threat was put to me last night or any other night.'

'Well it is early days. I will need to interview all of your staff and guests.'

'Yes of course, but we had a function here last night, a lot of people were about. If you include the ballroom, the bars, the dining room and the staff on duty there were probably over 200 people milling about. It was poison that killed him wasn't it?'

'We think it maybe so but we don't yet know what the poison was or how it was administered or even when he died. I should have the answers to those questions and a picture, later this morning, and then I will need to talk to you again. No doubt those answers will lead to more questions, meanwhile please ask Ian Witty to come to see me as soon as possible.'

I took that as a dismissal, and left the room to look for Ian.

With a wedding reception in the hotel that evening I was far too busy to ponder on the police interview for long but my tranquillity, if that is what it was, was rudely broken when I was directed to see D.C.I. Blake after only an hour or two. With considerable trepidation I trudged back to Room 26.

'We have found out,' D.C.I. Blake started, 'that Richard Jenkins had been poisoned, and that the poison had been administered from the open bottle of wine. Our experts found a small hole had been drilled along the length of the cork, just the size of a syringe needle.' D.C.I. Blake told me this in a bland very even voice, devoid of all emotion.

He pointed to a bottle of wine still standing on one of the hotel trays.

'Is this wine from your cellar?'

'It looks like it,' I said, 'my manager is the wine expert, I know we have a lot of French wine, and this includes red wine from the Rhone area in my cellars but my knowledge of wine is not great, naturally your colleagues may inspect my wine cellar if they wish to.'

'They already have, and have found several cases of wine from the Cotes-de-Rhone area, wine which had been bottled at that same Chateau.'

'Oh dear,' I was getting worried.

'My experts say it would take quite a little while to drill out a hole through the cork, and administer the poison, probably about half an hour. This would seem to put the murderer or murderess as someone with very close links with your hotel.'

'I don't quite follow you.'

'Somebody must have obtained the wine, prepared the poison, prepared the tray with the biscuits and have arranged for everything to be up here presumably before the deceased went to bed. The wine is a start, how could an outsider have managed to get the bottle from the cellar?'

'I cannot help you except to say that the cellar door is never kept locked. I leave all of the wine ordering to my manager who makes a hobby of selecting wines. He is in France now buying up stock for the hotel. He has a fine palate and knows a good wine from a poor one, you will have to wait until Monday to talk to him, he will be back by then, although it is just possible that he will call in on Sunday evening. Obviously the murderer could not have been him, he was out of the country.'

'How do you know he was abroad?'

'He told me he was going,' I said, it seemed feeble even to me.

'Well let us explore how the wine came to be in this room. I have asked your Gloria and she is adamant that the wine has not been booked to the room's account, so it was not brought up by your room service'.

'We don't really have a room service.'

'It must have been brought up by someone who had a pass key unless Richard Jenkins opened the door to the murderer himself, which seems unlikely. It would take a lot of nerve to deliver the spiked wine in person, suppose Jenkins had invited the person who delivered the wine, to take a drink with him. Incidentally, are these hotel biscuits?' the policeman asked me.

'Yes they look like the type of biscuits we have in the hotel bar.'

'And these are hotel glasses on a hotel tray?'

'Yes, that's right.'

'We have been making enquiries and have learnt a little more as to why Mr Richard Jenkins came to stay at the Bull this weekend and what he was doing generally. He was, it seems, a bit of a hard man, he had a knack of making people sell things they wanted to keep. He was not a subtle man, he used force. From enquiries of his past dealings we have found that he would beat up one or two of the staff, to make all the others leave. He would puncture all of the tyres on the vehicles in the car park, he would get fights started every night in the hotel bar. Windows would be broken continuously often using a catapult. Every night the fire alarm would go off waking everyone, causing mayhem. No guests would put up with that sort of thing, so the hotel would empty and eventually would become insolvent. Jenkins would buy the business at a knock down price; and surprise surprise, all of the misfortune would stop as soon as he took control. I am telling you this because it means you have motive to kill him, the means to kill him and you do not have an alibi.'

'I didn't know any of this and I don't need an alibi,' I said.

'Hmm, I have a photograph of him now, take a look, do you remember speaking to him or seeing him other than as a hotel guest?' said the policeman.

'Yes, the face does look vaguely familiar but he has never done business with me.'

'You agree you were around the hotel last night?'

'Of course I was, it's my hotel, I was on duty.'

'And you didn't see anyone or anything suspicious?'

'No, really I didn't.'

'Well, thank you for your assistance Miss White, I expect we will need to talk to you again later.'

I was very relieved to leave the room.

That Saturday afternoon and evening the hotel was the venue for a wedding feast. It was to start at 4 o'clock with tea and biscuits being served, something for the wedding guests to do while the remainder of the photographs were being taken and the bride and groom sorted themselves out, whatever that means. Then on to sherry, a sit down meal of prawn cocktail, chicken and chips, pavlova, wine with the meal, and Champagne with the wedding cake. Beer and wine was served with soft drinks available.

Not my personal choice of food but that is what the bride and groom, or to be more precise, the bride's mother, wanted to have and we were there to try to please the customers. Not always an easy task.

I checked the rosters of the staff who would be on duty that evening, and realised I could do with an extra pair of hand. Two of my regulars had telephoned in to say they were unwell, I suspect that the illness was political but that is the name of the game with temporary staff in hotels. I wondered who else I might call upon at short notice and thought of Rosemary. It was Rosemary that I had bumped into by the churchyard shops on the Thursday afternoon and she was the reason I had been late for my appointment and had had to rush back. Rosemary Parker was her full name, she had had problems with her son who, it seems, was taking drugs. I was sometimes called upon to offer a sympathetic ear. We had first met when Rosemary was a chambermaid for my parents five or six years previously and we had always got on although we are very different people. Then Rosemary, who had been taciturn, petulant, but efficient was chief chambermaid and ruled her small staff with a rod of iron, something I had never managed. My management style was to persuade and lead by inspiration rather than to bark out orders. Rosemary had told me she was in need of money, she would surely help out for the evening. I telephoned her and was startled by her abrupt rejection of the offer of an evening's employment. She seemed to infer that it was the last thing she needed. I felt a bit hurt, oh well, none so queer as folk. I had a long list of ladies, and a few gentlemen who sometimes leant a hand at serving or washing up. All paid cash of course.

The telephone rang, Charles was put through, he started to give me news of his morning but I had to cut him short, I really had so much to do.

'Sorry Charles, I have a small crisis on. I need another set of hands this evening to help out but I can't yet find anyone willing and able to come at such short notice, so I must make some more calls, may I ring you later?'

'I'll come and help,' he volunteered.

'Don't be silly,' said I, 'Why do I need an equine dentist at my hotel, give me a ring tomorrow, or I will telephone you.' I rang off a little abruptly I fear. Five calls later and I had managed to organise two additional waitresses. Just a little more help can make such a difference.

What also made a difference and what cheered me up no-end, was a huge bouquet of flowers delivered with a card inscribed 'Life's not meant to go too smoothly, there has to be a challenge to overcome, love Charles. Kisses.'

At 8.30 on that Saturday evening the hotel was once again buzzing. The wedding reception had been, still was, a great success. The bars were full, the guest rooms were all taken except for the one sealed by the police. The kitchen was past its mad fury and now was a gathering place for endless washing up. I was quite happy to help with any of the hotel tasks, from cleaning a lavatory to checking people in to washing up but I knew I had to be a figurehead. I walked from bar to function room to dining room to kitchen, where I saw the back of someone, who was certainly not one of my employees, washing up.

'Hello, what are you doing here?' I asked

'I think I am washing up,' said Charles.

'That's not quite what I meant,' I said smiling, 'And well you know it. Thanks so much for the flowers, they're truly beautiful.'

'You're most welcome. Incidentally do I get brownie points for the washing up?' he asked.

'We will have to see whether you are up to scratch,' I was secretly delighted, but I was not going to admit it to Charles. I walked off to see to other duties.

Sometime after 10 o'clock when I was alone in my office again, taking stock of things, there was a knock on the door. It was, of course, Charles.

'Sorry, below stairs staff cannot come in here,' I said.

'Damn cheek,' said Charles. 'Your huge volume of washing up has been done, it took ages. I like your dish washing machine, it's a bit like a car wash.'

A continuous dish washer had been installed by my parents just before they died. The operator stacked dishes into the machine at one end, on a system indeed much like a car wash, clean dry dishes appeared at the other end of the machine. Someone still had to put them away, but we had made even that task easier. We had standardised steel trays made up that fitted both the dishwasher and the storage unit. It was just a question of lifting the tray off the conveyor belt, and placing it in its position on the rack. The trays, when full of crockery, were quite heavy.

'I really am grateful,' I said. 'Come here you, I want to thank you.' I took him in my arms, and kissed him. 'What I would really like is a gentle walk,' I nearly added "before going to bed" but stopped myself saying that bit just in time. I certainly didn't mean it like that.

We let ourselves out of the hotel, I was still wearing my business clothes. We wandered over the bridge spanning the tiny river Hiz and walked hand in hand as it happened up towards the Three Moorhens Inn, across a footbridge and into open countryside. It was very dark, Charles put an arm around my waist and I put an arm around his waist.

'Look at that sky,' said Charles.

'All those stars.'

'And planets.'

'Which are the planets. I can't tell the difference.' I said.

'Let's see. That is Venus over there. Goddess of love, don't you know.'

'How do you know it's Venus?'

'Venus is easy,' said Charles. 'Venus is very big and

bright at present, and of course, Venus doesn't twinkle.'

'Twinkle twinkle little star.'

'Just so, not twinkle twinkle little planet.'

'It is all so far away,' I snuggled up against him, 'and you are so close.' We were walking very slowly.

'Love your scent,' said Charles.

We had been walking all this time, along a pathway just wide enough for two people, if they were friendly. I think it can be said we were being friendly. We paused, and Charles kissed me, then again. Then he nibbled my ear.

'Are you more relaxed?' he asked.

'My heart seems to be beating quite quickly.'

We walked on, even more slowly than before.

'I love the night when there is no moon.' said Charles in little more than a whisper.

'The sky is so clear. Why aren't there any stars over there?' I asked.

'The Hitchin street lights outshine the stars in that part of the sky.'

'I think I would rather have the stars.'

'Me too, but then most romantic people would,' said Charles.

Then to show how romantic I really was, I yawned.

'Time to get you back,' said Charles, we retraced our steps. At the hotel we let ourselves into the premises and returned to the manager's office I took Charles in my arms again. He started to caress me.

'No, no,' I said. 'Not here, I mustn't be the subject of hotel gossip. Let me think, if you are serious, go to the 4th floor, Room 43 in about ten minutes' and with that I led him to the door.

It was actually nearer 20 minutes before I was able to climb the four flights of stairs. I could have been there a bit sooner but decided a little delay might not go amiss. I found Charles looking out of the window pretending not to hear me. I crept up behind him and pretended to surprise him but of course he knew I was there. I put my arms around him nestling my cheek against his back.

'Why did you come to wash up tonight?'

'I came to see you, the washing up was a ruse, as you well know.'

'And what do you want of me?'

'Now let me think, you are good at running an hotel, are you good at anything else?'

'What sort of thing else?' asked I.

'Lessons in, kissing,' said Charles.

'You don't need kissing lessons from me!'

'Is that a statement or a question?'

'Are you still trying to flirt with me?' said I.

'I thought I was succeeding.'

'Gosh I am tired.'

'Lie down,' said Charles, 'let me massage your back but first for heaven sake take off your jacket. Why do you wear a jacket on a night as hot as this?'

Chapter 2

'It's my uniform,' I slipped the jacket off my shoulders and undid the top two buttons of my blouse.

'Here let me do that,' said Charles, he slowly undid the remaining four buttons and let the white blouse slip to the floor. 'Lie down,' he ordered, 'lie on your front.'

Obediently, why did I obey him? I lay down, first slipping off my shoes, but I did feel incongruous wearing my long black skirt with my tiny lace bronze coloured bra. Charles slipped the catch on my bra and stroked my back first with his hands then covering my flesh with tiny kisses sending shivers up my back.

He patted my bottom.

'Turn over,' he said, so I did letting my bra fall off my chest. He took one of my nipples between his fingers and kissed me on the lips, first a peck, then getting more and more intense. He straddled me, holding one of my small breasts in each hand, continuing to kiss me; the bed was creaking so much that we both started laughing.

'He ran his fingers down the side of my body catching the top of my black skirt, finding the side zip, he released its hold and tried to draw the skirt from my hips but it was much too tight.

'Your bum is too big, I need some help,' said Charles.

'Its not big, I'm only size 12. I thought you were an expert,' I said raising my middle off the bed and giving a little wiggle. Underneath I wore a thong made of bronze lace.

'So here I am, wearing only a tiny thong, and you are

fully dressed even wearing shoes. Get them off!'

'Is this the modest proprietor of the Bull Hotel,' said Charles.

'A lady takes her modesty off with her petticoats. I think these shoes of yours can come off, and socks yes' I really manhandled him 'yes this shirt and certainly these trousers, and those underpants, there that's better.'

'But now I am wearing nothing except a smile, and you are still wearing a thong. Come here you.'

Charles slipped a finger either side of my waist, and pulled my thong down to my knees, then onto the floor.

'Why don't you sit on my knee,' said Charles, so I did, lowering my bare bottom onto him. He put one arm around my waist while the other played with my breasts and nipples. Perhaps I should have objected, but I didn't.

'Why do you want me to sit on your knee?'

'Perhaps I want to talk.'

'To talk!!'

'That's the trouble with women, always want to rush things, never time to ...'

I jumped up, grabbed both of Simon's wrists. he stood up too, and we started fighting, then fell back onto the creaking bed into each other's arms, and into each other's bodies, neither of us cared how much the bed squeaked.

❧ CHAPTER 3 ❧

That Sunday morning I woke up at about 7.30 to the sound of church bells ringing from St Mary's Church about half a mile away and to the sight of Charles gazing at me or to be more precise, at those parts of my body that were not covered by my bed clothes. A lot of me was exposed.

'Morning darling,' he said. 'Sleep well?'

'Mmm how long have you been awake?' I asked.

'Oh about half an hour, you look so pretty asleep, it's a lovely morning. I am free today, I would suggest that we go for a long walk after breakfast but I expect you're going to be really busy, not least because the police will want to interview you again.'

'Yes sorry, I would have loved to have spent the day with you but my hotel duties call and I must get ready to go back to Colchester University.' Charles bent over and kissed me gently, then slowly nibbled at one of my ears.

'Do you think we can find an hour or two to spend together today?' he whispered.

'Together together alone, or together together with other people?'

'Together together alone could be interesting but supposing we ran out of things to say to each other.'

'We could read.'

'Read minds, books, bodies?'

'Or we could think.'

'Talking about thinking, Jenkins, bless him and how to find out who killed him. If he has taken over businesses previously in the same way as he was going to try to make you sell the Bull to him, and I think that is what you said the police suggested, then all of those people he defrauded are possible murderers. If we could get a list of all of their businesses, it would be a start.'

Charles was saying this at the same time as he played with my pubic hair. I had some small difficulty in concentrating on what he was saying to me.

'But I have no idea how to get a list,' he added.

'At University, we do have,' I said, gently pushing away his hand and turning in bed so my back was towards him, 'A data base of every person who has, over the last 20 years, been a shareholder or director in any company in England and Wales. I could make a search against Jenkin's name, and the names of all the members of his immediate family.'

Charles muzzled up to my back, kissing my spine whilst sliding one of his hands between my thighs so that he could continue to play with my pubic hair, this time even more intimately.

'Good idea, it could be a way forward, to see if any members of Jenkins's close family have bought any companies in the last few years,' he said. He was still fondling me, I either had to make a move immediately or it would be another half hour or so.

'I must shower,' I said making a real effort, 'You can soap

my back if your really want to, then I must get on.'

Accepting my invitation with alacrity, he soaped me all over, kissed bits of me here and there which he seemed to find particularly interesting and then slipped himself into me giving me one mighty kiss at the same time, all the while the warm water cascaded down onto our naked bodies. It certainly was one of the better ways of getting clean. Phew!

I dressed carefully in a business suit and walked downstairs, the demur proprietress once again, leaving Charles already fast asleep. Sunday was his day off, he was not a church goer, he looked pretty good asleep, but then he looked pretty good awake as well. I gave him a peck on the cheek, but he didn't notice. Downstairs I checked each of the public rooms of the hotel, checked that the staff on duty had as few problems as possible, went over to the computer to consider the bookings for the week, which were not too bad and had some breakfast accompanied by the Sunday papers.

Over my breakfast of coffee and toast I thought about Charles' plan of how we might collate a list of suspects. It was the only plan we had, so to make a start I considered how we could get the names of the various members of Jenkin's family. And then I thought of Gloria.

Gloria was not on duty that morning, so immediately after leaving the dining room I broke one of my golden rules and telephoned her at home. Gloria had been born and been to school in Hitchin; she had the knack of knowing scores of people, many more than me and she had the delightful habit of keeping in touch with her acquaintances. I asked her if she knew the Jenkins family but she didn't and my hopes were dashed, never-the-less I explained my interest. She said she thought she might know someone who could help and rang off. Sure enough after only about 15 minutes, Gloria telephoned back reporting the results of her various efforts, she sounded quite excited.

'Lucy,' she said, 'it was easier than I thought it would be. I telephoned a friend who knows the Jenkins and really wanted to gossip. She had heard of the murder and already knew that I worked at the Bull, she told me the whole family history, with names and even ages of the children. I think I have all the information you might need and will bring the details in with me tomorrow if that is OK.'

I thanked her warmly. 'You are wonderful,' I said.

'Yes I am,' she said. I could feel her smile down the telephone it was so strong.

Strangely, at least I thought it was strange, the police seemed in no hurry to talk to me again, that suited me fine. They had interviewed every member of my staff they could rustle up but I didn't know the answers they were given. One or two of my staff seemed to be giving me furtive looks, but it may have been my imagination, I was probably getting paranoia. I asked if I could have Room 26 back into circulation but they said no, not for several days, so that was that. I turned to sorting out what I would need in

Colchester and buried myself for a while in English History, no great hardship for me.

I had long since made a schedule of each of William the Conqueror's followers, and wanted to track their descendants down the ages, trying to find something new to put in my thesis. I had a great deal of reading to do, the day wore on. Charles, bless him, was kind enough to attend to some odd jobs around the hotel, a curtain rail in one room, a sticking door in another, a bar stool which wobbled when sat on. We were unable to go riding as the owners of the horses were taking them out themselves. In the end I suggested a walk.

We drove out to the village of Weston which is about four miles east of Hitchin. I'm constantly surprised by the reaction of people living outside the county, they are amazed by the number of really picturesque Hertfordshire villages that exist each with its own charm, often with very good community spirit. Charles knew them all from having visited stables throughout the area in the course of his work. Weston is delightful. We parked by the Cricketers Pub, walked a hundred yards or so, through two gates and we were in open countryside with extensive views over Hertfordshire and Bedfordshire. Tucked between the trees one could just see the four top storeys of Lister Hospital again. We walked half a mile, cows on one side and a field of stubble on the other, until we came to a large wood. Apart from the birds, it was very quiet.

'In the spring time the floor of this wood is carpeted with bluebells, it's fantastic, but then there are countless bluebell woods in North Hertfordshire, I don't know about the rest of the county.'

'I have never been here; I tend to visit the stables in the area, then head back to the main road to get my next appointment,' said Charles looking around at the variety of huge trees which surrounded him. 'I wonder how many pairs of eyes are looking at us at this moment? Can you hear that bird? I think it's a blackbird but ornithology isn't one of my strong points. I saw a tree creeper the other day, I would not have known what it was if I hadn't had a friend with me who was a bit of an expert. Did you know there are many herds of wild deer in North Hertfordshire, I don't know if they ever come up here. I think I would if I were a deer.'

'You are a dear, dear.'

'Thank you dear.' We both giggled.

Charles kissed me under the branches of a giant tree, I don't know what sort of tree, it didn't matter greatly, our attention was elsewhere. I think Charles would have liked a proper cuddle but I didn't want to be automatically available to him. I then wondered if I was playing power games and if I was, whether it was a good thing or a bad thing. Spare me from psychology.

'Let me tell you,' he said as we walked out of the wood towards the hamlet of Chesterfield 'about an hotel I stayed at with a young lady a year or two ago. It was on the Newcastle road way up north.

We had driven up north, one Thursday evening, not expecting any trouble in finding an hotel where we might stay a few days, but parking in Newcastle was impossible and too soon we found ourselves driving right through the city and out of the other side. Fortunately, after about half an hour's drive, we came across an hotel at the side of the road, with a large empty car park. It looked a pleasant enough place so we stopped, parked up and walked into the reception area.

The gentleman behind the desk looked up at us and considered our request for accommodation for three or four nights. He said he could give us breakfast but not evening meals. That suited us fine and we accepted. The man then went off, we had to call him back and ask him which room we should have.

'Take your choice,' said mine host, waving at the full key board, so we selected a really pleasant room at the head of quite a grand flight of stairs. It had a bathroom en suite a lovely view, and bright decor. For supper we had a Chinese meal. Driving back we saw that the hotel was in darkness, we felt very sorry for the owner, obviously the hotel was losing money, he needed to do something to attract clientele. As soon as we entered the doorway the owner saw is in, locked up and went off, presumably to bed. We went to bed straight away.'

'I bet you did,' I said.

'Waking up early next morning,' Charles said, ignoring me, 'We found the hotel still in darkness. It was a lovely morning so we drew back the curtains, unbolted the door and went for a walk, returning very hungry. As we were having breakfast, another couple drove up and asked for accommodation. The owner just said 'No'. He gave no reason, did not say he was full up, or closed, he just said 'No!'

The couple said, 'then can we just have breakfast we are really hungry?' watching us eating our meal.

The owner said, 'no you can't.'

'Well they are,' said the couple pointing at us.

'Well you can't,' said the owner and walked away.

Immediately we stopped feeling sorry for the owner, if he were turning away paying guests he didn't deserve sympathy but we wondered why would he behave like that. To cut a long story short, we drove off spending the day walking over Hadrians Wall I think it was, returning to the hotel after we had had our supper. We expected the hotel to be in darkness again, but we couldn't have been more wrong.

The car park was full. The roads either side of the car park were lined with cars. Inside the hotel, three large bars had been opened with seven or eight barmaids. There was really loud music, people drinking and eating everywhere, the whole place was lively, vibrant, almost wild. The owner caught sight of us and bought us both a drink telling us it might be a bit noisy for an hour yet. We said we didn't mind, what else could we say.

After about half an hour we went to bed, but couldn't snuggle up. Every few minutes one of the ladies would knock on the door to ask if she could use the loo. It seems the queue at the various toilets was a bit long, and some were desperate, it's very off-putting hearing a stranger having a pee in the next room.'

I listened intently to Charles's tale. I am always interested in how other people run their hotel, how they cope with the vast workload and the often itinerant staff. I am always willing to learn, but cannot see the Bull adopting the tactics that evidently pay off near Newcastle.

Returning to the Bull I bumped into my manager Martin Lynch, who, whilst looking in rude health, also looked very perplexed. He was a man in his late forties, very very good at his job. He had a knack of making things work, not gadgets but people, functions, rotas, hotel life. If a customer had had a little too much to drink, Martin would humorously get the man to call it a day. If a waitress had a grouse, Martin would sense it and sort it out before it became a problem. If a guest was upset, Martin could smooth them over. I asked him once why he didn't choose to manage a larger more prestigious hotel in a city, he explained that he had done that and it was stressful. At the Bull Hotel, his input really counted: he was in charge of the wine cellars which he loved, he had free time almost when he wanted it, London was only half an hour away by train, and the work was enjoyable. Here was Martin, back from his holidays in France, a most welcome face.

'Our wanderer has returned, Martin, it is good to see you. Thank you for your card, did you really have a wonderful time?'

'Hello Lucy,' he said. 'It's good to see you too. Yes I had a most pleasant break but have just had my session with the police so the homecoming left a little to be desired. A good hour and a half I spent with them, the questions they asked me; did I know you were going to be taken over? Are you? Had we had an argument? Did I know the deceased? Did I know that poisoning was often a woman's crime? Can I prove I was abroad? And did a bottle of wine come from the hotel cellars?'

'The wine did, didn't it, I have served wine bearing just that label myself in the dining room,' I said. 'In fact I have served it many times.'

'You have no doubt served one similar, but not a year 1993. That was a dreadful year, you have probably served a 1995 from the same vineyard.'

'Sorry, you have lost me. I know so little about wine.'

'That will have to be remedied, it is truly a fascinating subject, but we digress. The bottle the police showed me, the one that was supposed to contain the poison, was produced in 1993, when there was a glut of very poor quality wine. The wine I bought for the hotel, several dozen bottles, was produced in 1995 a much better year but a year which did not produce the quantity. We have never had any 1993 wine in the hotel cellars, I promise you that the two years are like chalk and cheese.'

'So there is no chance of the bottle of wine containing the poison having come from the hotel cellars?' I was relieved, and no doubt it showed in my face.

'No possibility at all, but you can buy the 1993 wine almost anywhere. It is readily available in the off licences and supermarkets, it's a bit cheap and cheerful.'

'And you told the police all of this?' I asked.

'Yes of course I did.'

'And they believed you?'

'They had no choice, I don't think that D.C.I. Blake knows any more about wine than you do.'

'He thinks I murdered the man.'

'I don't think he really does, a bit too obvious.'

'Well who did?' I asked.

'Now there you have me.'

'The man is dead.'

'That is true.'

'Martin I am so glad that you are back. Did you really have a good time?'

'Fantastic! I want to persuade you to buy some cases of Crozes Hermitage, it is some very good red wine I found'

'Have you already bought it?' I asked. I must admit I

was a bit suspicious. Sometimes Martin's enthusiasm stops him being commercial, I had to make sure the hotel made a profit from each bottle.

'Yes just a couple of cases or so, but wait until you taste it, then we can give a proper order. How is the hotel doing?' he said changing the subject.

'Apart from Room 26 all is very well. At the wedding reception on Saturday they got through a vast amount of beer, I think it was partly the heat, it was very warm that day. The charity function on Thursday was first class and there they drank your wine by the gallon, they must have made quite a hole in your cellars.

'What fun,' Martin's eyes gleamed, 'perhaps we should make a few more purchases, I have made so many contacts over the last few weeks.'

I love it when someone is enthusiastic about their job and Martin was certainly that, although looking after the wine cellar was just a small part of his work.

'This visit I restricted myself to just one area of France rather than dash all over the place. I drove to Gevrey Chamertin near Dijon and explored from there. I drove all over the Cote de Nuit the Cote de Beaune and the Cote Chalonnaise, fascinating.

I visited one cave in the morning and another in the afternoon, that way I could do them justice. Each visit lasted about two and a half hours what with discussing things. As I am doing it for the hotel, what do you say that

I count it as part of my duties and don't take it as holiday?'

'Martin, I know that I am young, I may be inexperienced, but I am not that green. I am pleased you had a good break though. Welcome back to this crazy place, I am really glad that the wine was the wrong year.

Is that the reception bell ringing? I had better see what is the problem.'

I left Martin and walked out into reception where I found a somewhat irate middle-aged gentleman walking up and down.

'I am so sorry to keep you sir,' I said.

'About time too, I have been waiting ages, I thought you must all have gone to sleep. My name is Abraham, I have a reservation here for two nights.'

'Ah yes, Room 10, would you please sign the register; there is the key sir, shall I get someone to help you with your luggage?'

'No I can manage, I am not quite that old yet' and he walked off towards the lift. It was Ian who should have been on reception duty; I would have to find out why he wasn't doing his job properly. I made a quick search for him, and found him in my office, just staring in front of him.

'Ian,' I said, 'didn't you hear the reception bell?' Ian didn't move a muscle, he seemed in a daze. I spoke to him again and touched his arm, 'Ian, what is the matter?'

He mumbled something that I could not catch. I asked him again.

'They think I did it,' he said at last.

'Did what?'

'Murdered Jenkins.'

'They thought I had done it this morning,' I said, 'The police are just floundering about seeing who might be caught in the net.'

'No, no, they really believe it was me. I expect to be arrested quite soon. I had motive, opportunity, intent, and no alibi, they are sure it was me.'

'Why should it be you?' I asked.

'Because that miserable sod ruined my father,' said Ian.

'Say again.'

'Bloody Jenkins, the murdered man, ruined my father. He made my father sell his business for a derisory sum and it almost destroyed him. I hated Jenkins, have done for almost a year. If I had had the chance, I would have killed him.'

'But you didn't know he was staying at the hotel.'

'Oh yes I did. I took the original telephone booking from him, I checked him in. I was so angry I mixed up the keys if you remember. I was even planning how I could do it but my idea was to bash him on the head.'

'Did you murder him?'

'No. No I didn't, but the police are sure I did,' said Ian.

'Heavens what a web. Did you know that the wine that carried the poison didn't come from the hotel cellar after all?'

'Yes the police told me but they also said it can be bought

in many shops in Hitchin. They are piecing together bits and pieces and they all point to me.'

'Ian, as a start, for me, write down what you did for every minute of Thursday evening; exactly where you were, and who you were with. Do it as soon as possible but do it really carefully.'

'You mean to see if I do have some sort of alibi, I suppose it might help, thanks.'

I walked back to reception, it appeared I would be on reception duty for that evening, Ian's mind wasn't on the job. I had fancied a cuddle with Charles but he would have to slip off soon after 8 o'clock as he was horse sitting that evening; that's business and business usually must come first. Now how could I make it up to Charles next time we meet. I would have to think of something special.

Yet Sunday night was always the slackest evening of the week, very few people were staying, and the restaurant was almost empty. I decided to do some detective work, if I did not kill Jenkins, and Ian did not kill him, someone else did. That person must have had a motive and the opportunity to produce the spiked wine bottle, put it on a tray, add a glass or two, add a biscuit or two, and take it up to Room 26 with a pass key. Then undo the door when they knew Jenkins was not there, leave the wine, and retreat, all without being noticed. A tall order, not necessarily because it could not be done but because the person could not rely on being able to do it secretly. The whole thing must have been planned carefully, it would have been impossible to build into the plan the chance of not being seen. The murderer must have appreciated that he or she would be noticed but had acted in such a way that it would not matter.

Jenkins checked into his room at about 3 pm. Until he was given his keys the murderer could not be sure which room he would be given, rooms were often changed at the last minute to accommodate guests' particular fancies. The only person who might have been able to wangle the key change was Ian and that point must have occurred to the police. I didn't go a bundle on D.C.I. Blake, but he was certainly no fool. The wine bottle could not have been taken up before 3 pm, but it could have been delivered almost any time after that until the man died; which Martin had been told was estimated by the police at sometime shortly after midnight. That gave nine hours, such a long time to account for toings and froings. A complicating feature of laying a trap, which in essence this was, is that the trap could have been laid over a period of many hours.

It then struck me that the chambermaid who turned down the sheets for guests, may have noticed the tray. It was Gillian who had been on duty that evening, she would be coming on duty that Sunday evening as well. Gillian was a bright girl who had a full time job away from the hotel as a secretary to one of the local solicitors. Her only function at the hotel was to turn down the bed linen in the evenings and in the winter, to draw the curtains. She refused to help wash up, or clean the rooms or serve behind the bars. Five evenings a week, Monday, Tuesday, Wednesday, Thursday and Sundays she came through the rear door, put on a uniform, went around all the occupied rooms preparing them for the night, changed out of her uniform, and left. I hardly ever saw her. She was efficient, quiet, reliable. She refused to do Friday and Saturday nights.

I walked to the rear of the hotel, keeping an ear for the reception bell, and met Gillian almost as soon as she arrived. We had always got on quite well, but it was as employer employee although I think we could have been friends under different circumstances.

'Gillian,' I said. 'A word please.'

'Hello Lucy,' she said. 'Is there something wrong?'

I led Gillian to the manager's office and sat her down.

'You will have heard about Mr Jenkins dying in Room 26.'

'I should think the whole town knows about it, if not the whole county.'

'I have been trying to piece things together, not with much success and I wondered if you would cast your mind back to last Thursday when you did the room in the evening.'

'The police have already asked me.'

'Surely but just humour me, do you recall what time you did that room?'

'It would have been about 9.30 pm. I started work at

9 o'clock, by the time I reached Room 26, it would have been about half an hour later. The police asked me whether I had seen the bottle of wine in the room and I said that I was certain that it wasn't there and I am still certain that it wasn't there at 9.30.'

'Did you see anyone around the hotel, perhaps looking furtive or different, or lost?'

'You mean did I see Ian wearing a chambermaid's outfit running upstairs?'

The thought made me smile. 'Something like that.'

'Absolutely not. Nothing at all strange whilst I was around.'

'Thank you kindly, sorry to have delayed you.'

Things were looking up. I now had a span of two and a half hours, say from 9.30 to midnight during which time the bottle on the tray must have been delivered, always providing Gillian herself was not the murderess and that the bottle was not in the room when she entered and did the bed for the night. She might just not have noticed the tray, it seemed unlikely though.

Ian came in with the schedule of what he had done, and where he had been that fateful evening. To say that it was of little use was an under estimate. He had been on reception until 8 o'clock. He then had half an hours supper break, going back on duty until 11 o'clock when he went home. It would have been difficult for him to have taken up the tray whilst he was on reception duty, which left the hour from the time he came off duty, to the time Jenkins was killed.

I asked Ian whether anyone could vouch for him at home, but drew a blank. He lived not far away and although his parents saw him, they could not remember at what time it was that they saw him. They had no reason to note the time, they were watching television all evening but what they were watching didn't sink in.

Unhappily it was beginning to look like an inside job. Really anyone connected with the hotel could have done it and over the years we had employed a host of temporary and part-time staff. I was glad that I was not in D.C.I. Blake's shoes.

Nevertheless it was hardly a problem I could ignore. I poured myself out a cup of coffee and sat alone pondering the effect it might have on the hotel's trade, whether I could do anything about it and whether it was fair to leave the problem in Martin's lap.

I decided that, looking at things as objectively as I could, he was probably in a better position to deal with the problem being totally above suspicion himself, a good bit older than me, good at smoothing out difficulties, and although I hated to admit it would make any difference, male. The police seemed to give him a little more respect than they gave me. It was time I changed from hotel proprietor to student.

❧ CHAPTER 4 ❧

I am not sure why, for I am not really ashamed of it but I don't advertise the fact that I own and ride a 600 cc motor bike. A red Suzuki. I seldom use it in Hitchin but usually travel back to Colchester on it and I always used it around the University. Motor bikes have such a poor reputation; yet they are a wonderful mode of transport, exhilarating ,fascinating to drive, easy to park, and use hardly any petrol. Why everyone doesn't own one I can't imagine. Bikes can be driven dangerously, indeed they often are, but they need not be.

Early Monday morning, just four days after the murder, I dressed in my motorcycle gear of black boots, black trousers, black jacket, silver helmet and black gloves. I walked to the garage, wheeled out my bike and set off down Tilehouse Street, up to the Three Moorhens roundabout, along the Stevenage road, all in fourth gear, running at about 4,000 revs and 30 miles an hour. Along the duel carriageway stretch I opened her up to pass a car increasing my revs and speed before slowing down for the roundabout. Down to second gear, check it is clear, then up onto the motorway slipway bring the accelerator back, climb to 7,000 revs checking the traffic on the motorway and making sure it is safe. The acceleration is amazing. Along the motorway, off at the next junction into Baldock then, turning right along the A507 to Buntingford now thankfully by passed, onto the A10 and A120.

Motor cycling is so unlike driving a car, for a start the motorcyclist is so vulnerable, no safety belt, the crumple zone is your own body, two wheels not four, cold toes, no heater. Obvious but not always appreciated by car drivers. It pays to be very careful, it's a bit like skiing, endless exhilaration, effortless travel, but dangerous for the unwary. A motorcyclist approaching another motorcyclist, nods in greeting but never never nods to a scooter or moped rider. Shopping can be difficult, I remember riding without a saddlebag once, popping into the supermarket for a few odds and ends, but buying a little too much. I stuffed things down my front and in pockets, and ended up sitting on a tin of tomatoes. Not to be recommended at all.

It takes about an hour and a half to drive from Hitchin to Colchester, a pleasant drive on a bike, unless raining or very cold. Around Stansted Airport it can get a bit noisy, otherwise it is straightforward if a little ponderous. Even for a motor bike it can be a slow road because of the volume of traffic and the state of the surface. Parking for cars is not easy at the Campus but for a bike it is not at all a problem, just stop. I parked up, collected my pannier bag and walked to my rooms.

Graduates at Colchester University have small but acceptable accommodation, usually in a block containing only graduate rooms. We share kitchen, and sometimes bathroom facilities, there are rules about what we can and cannot do, we cannot paint our rooms for example. The rooms are adequate that's about all. Many graduates prefer to rent a flat or a room off campus in the city itself but I prefer to be on site. I like the sense of belonging, I enjoy the various facilities, the gym, the library, the computer laboratory, the common room. I meet more people at the campus, I feel in the middle of things especially sport facilities and computer laboratories.

I arrived at Colchester in high spirits, I usually did unless I was very cold or very wet. I'm not sure why this should be, perhaps it's the exhilaration of the ride, perhaps shaking off the responsibilities of the hotel, leaving the problems on someone else's shoulders. It is like having two separate identities, on the one hand the proprietor of a small hotel dealing with staffing, cash flow, bookings, and on the other hand the life of a student albeit the life of a graduate student with a deadline to handle a thesis, examinations and projects. There is also the other side of university life, parties, discussion, a bit of drinking, some people take drugs, masses of sport and student life generally. There is a great deal of reading to do, communication with other members of the college is usually through e-mails, it is a tight-knit community. My two lives are far apart.

I remember meeting an American who had served in the Vietnam war where the contrasts were extreme. He said that one moment he was in the hell hole of the front line, fearful for his life, actually killing people, the next he was eligible for

R & R and he was transported to the flesh pots of Hong Kong, just an hour or two away. I have always liked the concept of extremes in close proximity, the ocean liner with advanced electronics and French cuisine moored off a deserted island with coconuts and just the wind.

Almost as soon as I returned to Colchester, before I even unpacked properly or made myself a cup of tea, I called on a friend, Matthew Cooper. I had originally met Matthew in my first year at the university, we were in the same block of rooms together, and met at our first exploratory venture in the Student's Union bar. He was alone, I was alone, we got chatting and had never really stopped. He was good company, great fun, a member of the University Rugby Club, sometimes we jogged together but he was much faster than I could ever be. He had flirted with me on and off for almost the whole time we had known each other but we had never slept together only indulging in relatively innocent tumbles after various parties. Matthew like me, was now reading for his masters degree and had, under his control, a huge database giving, among other things, information on English and Welsh companies. It was this that I wanted to make use of.

Dumping my things on the bed, I glanced at my reflection in the mirror and was aghast at the disarray caused by my helmet and a 70 mile per hour wind. I grabbed a comb and some powder to help me repair some of the damage done by the journey. Perhaps it's obvious after all why many people prefer cars. I took what I call my leathers off, slipped on a skirt and left the room.

It took me just a little while to track Matthew down, when I had run him to earth I gave him an outline of what I wanted, that is, I showed him the list of names which Gloria had given to me and asked him if it were possible to match the names on that list with any of the names of his database. Then we could see if any of the people on Gloria's list had owned shares in any English company over the last few years. It seems that his database went back over a six year period. Kindly without even asking why, Matthew agreed to see if his computer could find any matches and promptly scanned Gloria's list into his computer, pressed a key or two and then suggested that we leave it for a while, have a coffee and return in due course to see what was picked up.

It struck me that Matthew might expect a favour in return but I was emphatic that it would not be the favour that Matthew wanted it to be. We went for our coffee.

'Is this seat taken?' I asked him as we entered the coffee shop.

'If it was taken, it wouldn't be there,' said Matthew, enacting an old ritual, silly really but we both smiled, sat down and ordered our drinks, coffee for each of us, and a flapjack. I paid.

'It's really good to see you,' I said to him. 'It must be five months or so since we last met. What have you been up to?'

'Apart from being celibate I've had quite an exciting time,

as you know I went to America, I spent much of the time in Arizona, at the University at Phoenix on an internship, Arizona's an amazing place.

'I have never been to the States,' I said.

'Nor had I before this visit, except once with my parents, for a weekend in New York, long, long ago when I was a child, but that was for shopping. I don't think I bought anything this time.'

'Did you tour around much?'

'I hired a car for most of the time, just a small Ford, but it served my purpose well, thankfully it had air conditioning, I think nearly all cars do out there. On one occasion I drove up to Grand Canyon, a long, long drive, all done at the regulation 60 miles per hour. The Grand Canyon is very grand.'

'Good heavens is it really, that is surprising, grand you say.'

'On the way back,' he said, ignoring my sarcasm, 'I drove to a town called Kingman on Route 66, where for some curious reason I visited a launderette and used up all of my quarters to get some clean clothes. Had lunch in an American diner served by the world's largest waitress, drove through the desert where they have world record hours of sunshine, but seem to make little use of solar electricity. I had a conducted tour around the majestic Hoover Dam, and lost a dollar or two in Las Vegas.'

'Everyone I've ever met who has been to Las Vegas has lost a dollar or two. Was it just Arizona you visited?'

'Actually Las Vegas is in Nevada but that's being pedantic. No, I stopped off in Chicago for two days on the way out, and in South Carolina at a place called Myrtle Beach for four days on my way back. That made a very pleasant break, I found American people so friendly, such fun.

'I had a friend who was a lifeguard for a season in South Carolina. She said one of her duties was to clear the water when there was a shark about.'

'Yes that's right, they blow a whistle and everyone must get out of the water.'

'How do you know when it's safe to get back in the water?'

'That's easy, they tell us.'

'Exactly, but how do the lifeguards know the water is safe?'

'They probably have access aerial reconnaissance.'

'No, no. Nothing so sophisticated. They just look and when they think it might be clear, when, in other words they think the sharks have swam off, they give the green flag a wave.'

'But sharks are often submerged, you cannot always see their fins.'

'Quite. You see my point. She had to rescue people too. It was a bit daunting for her, swimming in sea which she thought contained numerous sharks, going up to someone who is thrashing about in the water.'

'Mmm, most people seem to survive. Incidentally you ride don't you. I spent a few days horse riding on a ranch in Arizona, way out in the desert, we cantered down washes, found a rattlesnake, it was wild country,' said Matthew. 'Apart from that and apart from a lot of sport, I haven't done much recently. How about you?'

'Ah, yes a problem or two,' I said. 'In particular we had a murder at the hotel and it is in connection with the murder that I rushed over to see you.'

'A real murder!' he said, he was quite excited. 'I nearly said a real live murder, tell me more, what a thing to happen.'

'Yes, and I am very worried that business may suffer at the Bull. Who would want to stay at an hotel where the chances are you won't wake up in the morning?'

'I think you underestimate people's ghoulish sense of humour, it will probably increase your trade one hundred per cent and you'll end up having murder mystery weekends.'

'Now there's a thought.'

I brought Matthew up to date with events in Hitchin, Richard Jenkins being murdered in Room 26, the spiked wine, the problems as to how it reached the room. I told him the reason for Jenkins staying at the hotel, that he was going to threaten me and make me sell my interest in the Bull for a knock down price, and I told him that I was trying to get a clearer picture of what had happened.

'So you see Matthew,' I said, 'The fact is that in all probability he had used coercion previously. It was very unlikely that this would have been his first venture into making people sell their businesses at a very low price. If we could find out in what companies he or members of his family had held shares over the past few years, it might identify someone with a grudge big enough to wish him ill.'

We walked back to the computer laboratory and Matthew collected the paperwork. I had expected one or two sheets, but there were pages and pages of closely printed names. List after list as only computers seem able to provide; lists of companies of all descriptions, most were internationally or at least nationally known, big retailers, oil companies, construction firms; it seemed my ruse had not worked. Jenkins could not have threatened those big corporations.

We poured over the huge printout in silence.

'What we have,' said Matthew after a while, 'are numerous smallish investments. Most of this data is irrelevant for your purposes. All it proves is that the Jenkins' family have considerable share portfolios; it looks like he invested the proceeds of his take-overs, and any other money he had, in the stock market with as wide a range of stock as he could cover, presumably to hedge his bets, or not look obtrusive. Let's run the programme again, this time deleting any company that has a stockmarket listing and also any company with over fifty shareholders.'

'Can you do that?'

'We can try.'

After waiting a while Matthew produced an additional printout, this time much smaller, much more manageable. Gone were the nationals and multi nationals, left was a list of firms, none of which struck a cord with me. Now we had a list hopefully of all the companies in which Jenkins and members of his close family had had an interest. We could also print off a list of the directors and shareholders of those same companies before Jenkins became involved in them; our idea was that one of those names would be the murderer.

Matthew gave me the printout, I thanked him, ignored his eye but kissed him on the forehead and took the paperwork back to my rooms. I made myself a coffee and read and re-read through the list. I was far from certain how to proceed from there; it's not easy to go up to someone and say, you are on my list of possible murderers, prove it wasn't you. The only name I recognised was Ian Witty's family, and that hardly helped to prove it wasn't him.

After pouring over the new list I decided that I had spent quite enough of my time trying to solve what appeared to be the unsolvable; I gave up for the time being on the murderer or murderess, and studied history for three solid hours. I was then hungry, stiff, and needed some exercise.

I nibbled at an energy bar, changed into shorts, and went for a jog. The campus is criss crossed with colour coded tracks and I chose an intermediate one. I do get a buzz from exercise, but I try not to take it to extremes. Some people I know spend hours every day in the gym, I think they must get a real high from it. I jog, but not too fast, this time I ran round the place for about 40 minutes alone, not meeting anyone I knew on more than a nodding acquaintance. After a shower and a change of clothes I arranged to meet up with a few girl friends. We met at the common room and drifted off to Cafe Mondo for a meal, a drink and a chat. There were five of us Jane, a delightful person, Pauline, usually a little depressed, Anna always the tease and Fiona who was newish to the group. In fact I caused quite a stir, we were all more or less talking at once when I happened to mention the murder, suddenly complete silence reigned, not just between the four of us, but over the whole room. I had to explain that at my hotel one of the guests had been poisoned, that I did not know who did it, or why, or the nature of the poison. They were intrigued, mind you, so was the whole room.

I was inundated with questions, they asked me exactly what I do at the hotel. I had always fought shy previously of mentioning my hotel, in case it appeared a bit swanky.

'I look after the hotel when my manager is away, which means making sure everything from the bars to the lavatories to the dining room are all kept up to scratch. When the manager is there, which is most of the time, I try to make sure that the hotel is running on the correct lines, doesn't run out of money, has enough staff, agree advertising, that sort of thing. I also try to make sure that nobody gets murdered.'

'How can you do this and do a masters degree,' asked Jane.

'It isn't all that difficult,' I said, 'But I couldn't do it without a manager, it's he who runs the place most of the time.'

'When do you study then?'

'I snatch an hour or so here and there. I read whilst on reception, there are long periods of inactivity, after lunch for example.'

It was good to be back on the campus, my girl friends made me feel young at heart. I mentioned Charles, described him and wondered what I could do with him when he came. Some very lurid proposals were put forward by my friends before I explained that I wanted a fairly local, interesting place to visit, not to re-write the kama sutra. They suggested visiting Constable Country which was nearby, so perhaps we would.

That evening I was invited to a party. Parties at universities are usually happy-go-lucky affairs, although I do tend to put on my gladrags and a bit of face paint. When I arrived at the venue, someone's rooms, there were heaving bodies, music was blearing out, one or two people already seemed the worse for drink. Nothing unusual there then. I nudged my way into the room, looked about me, found a corkscrew and an acquaintance in the kitchen where the noise was not quite so loud and people could chatter. I talked to her, we drifted into the sitting room again but she couldn't really hear what I was saying, and she talked to me, but what she said was a bit of a mystery. After a while we left the room, went into the corridor where I listened to snatches of conversations between people around me.

Someone was talking about drugs but only in a mild way, someone else thought she might be pregnant. One of the men was trying to chat up a strange looking lady who I had not seen before. His chat-up lines were dreadful but they seemed to be working on her. I heard him ask her what the best chat-up line she had ever heard was, putting the onus on her I thought, but then I was the bystander. I didn't get to bed until nearly three, quite where the time went is not easy to remember. I don't drink that much, I never take drugs, I know we chatted some more, had a bite to eat and at one time boogied for a while. Suddenly it was the small hours of the morning.

I walked to my rooms, got into bed. Got out of bed and went to the loo, got into bed, the light was still on but I still fell asleep and slept until nearly 10 o'clock. As I hadn't drunk very much I didn't have a hangover. I showered and tried to decide what to wear. My figure isn't too bad, I hate my thighs but the rest of me is more or less all right. My tits are a bit small but they will do, my hair could be better and perhaps I'll change it dramatically one day soon, but I cannot do much about my thighs except diet occasionally; perhaps I shouldn't wear shorts. I put on my long washed denim skirt, with a white blouse and denim jacket, and breakfasted, as usual, off dry toast and coffee.

So it was Tuesday, I went to the gym, attended a lecture, read, then read a little more. The day passed fairly slowly until 4 o'clock. Charles telephoned and we talked and talked but when we eventually rang off, I would have been hard-put to so say what we had talked about, save that he was proposing to come visiting on Thursday morning. Most of what we said was not very sensible anyway. It was good to hear from him; one of the advantages of being self employed as Charles was, is that time can be taken off when it is convenient. It would be really good to see him again.

Wednesday is sports day at most universities and Colchester is no exception. It has to be the same day everywhere so that the various teams can play each other, there is little point in Colchester wanting to play Norwich on Wednesday, and for Norwich to want to play Colchester on Tuesday. I play hockey, left wing. My initials being L W my first games mistress, as a joke, put me on the Left Wing and the position stuck.

I am only mediocre at hockey but it is really quite fun, I usually end up driving the team to the venue in one of the university minibuses. That Wednesday we were playing U.E.A. the University of East Anglia at Norwich. As usual I drove half the team there, two mini buses were going. We lost the game three-one, which was good for us. As always it is the home team that is responsible for providing eats and a drink but I had to keep to a cup of tea, then water, as I was driving. All in all it made a good day out, kept me fit, made me laugh and we had a natter. There is usually lots of teasing on the way home too. And then Thursday came.

It had started to rain on Wednesday evening, on Thursday

it poured, the weather had really broken. Water collected in a huge puddle where drains were partially blocked and became overwhelmed, flooding one of the squares. Everyone became camouflaged in plastic.

Charles rang and left a message to say he would be aiming to arrive at approximately 10 o'clock but that he might be a little late as the weather was so dreadful. I thought he had telephoned to say that what with the weather he would put off his visit to another time, thankfully I was wrong. It then struck me just how much I was looking forward to seeing him again, but what to wear, that age-old problem. In the end, after much consideration I decided to dress up for him, minimalistically. So I put on my one pair of suspender belts. Men are always meant to like suspender belts and stockings, personally I don't see it, too much upper thigh on view but there is no accounting for taste.

On this occasion I was not dressing for me but to excite him, the occasion demanded something special, so I wore my deep red suspender belt and stockings, my raincoat, a pair of shoes and nothing else.

I walked down to the car park in the pouring rain to meet Charles's old van, half wondering if he would arrive early and walk to meet me by a different route, we might miss each other. My fears were groundless, I arrived at the car park first, and was virtually hiding when he drew up. I was hiding not to tease him, but to try to keep a little out of the downpour, it did not succeed. I was drenched, it was as if someone had thrown a bucket of water over me, Charles in his van was bone dry.

'You look a bit wet,' he said smiling at me.

'You look very dry.'

'I think I am about to get very wet.'

He opened the van door, immediately his prediction proved correct. Very very quickly he became sodden, not least because as soon as he stood up I put my arms around him and gave him a long lingering kiss, or did he put his arms around me and give me a long lingering kiss, one or the other or a bit of each. We walked hand in hand, ignoring the rain, past the sports centre, across the square, past one of the lecture halls and to the block containing my rooms. As soon as the door was closed he took me in his arms and kissed me. He was wearing a vast, very wet gabardine riding coat, I undid the buttons on his coat and found, underneath he was wearing jeans, a shirt and a jumper. He undid the buttons on my very wet rain coat and found underneath I was wearing nothing.

Nothing, unless you count the suspender belt and the stockings. I think he appreciated my efforts. I know he appreciated my body but I wasn't going to let him touch me for a little while. Once the coats had been abandoned he could look, yet for a while that was all. I made him coffee and brushed bits of me against him shamelessly as I planted a plate of doughnuts on the table, but as soon as he touched me I smacked his hand away; it was fun.

After lingering over coffee, me not him, I made him stand against the door. I knelt down and slowly undid his zip, yes he was appreciating my attentions. I licked him, held his balls in my hand, and nibbled him up and down, very slowly. When I thought he was ready to come, naturally I stopped and stood up. Charles took my nipples, each between two fingers and kissed me again whilst I undressed him. He asked me to kneel on the floor, which I consented to do, leaving me vulnerable to the inevitable. He made love to me, and came to a climax really quickly. I suppose I asked for it, well I did ask for it. I stood up, brushed his lips with mine, and went to dress in the bathroom, I always think undressing is so romantic, but dressing can be banal.

I hid my frustration, making sure I was bright and cheerful, we donned our coats and headed for the common room to discuss Matthew's much reduced list and compared it with Gloria's list. There appeared to have been five previous relevant take-overs, details of which met the criteria of a good business being sold to Jenkins or his wife and then resold presumably at a profit. Ian's parents were prominent but of the other four we knew nothing.

'I think we should check up to see if any of the people whose names are on this list have ever taken rooms at the Bull,' said Charles.

'Don't you think we should first tell D.C.I. Blake of our findings?'

'Old ploddy?'

'Who?'

'D.C.I. Plod. Could we not do both, report to the police, and also continue our researches? It would be interesting to see if any of the people mentioned on the revised lists had stayed in the hotel, then there really would be a connection. Why not telephone Martin at the hotel now?'

From the common room I telephoned my manager Martin, getting through at the third try and after the usual pleasantries and after tasting his dry sense of humour I explained where we were with the various lists and told him what we wanted him to do.

He readily agreed, promising to match the lists produced by Matthew against the hotel register over the last few months and to telephone back as soon as possible. This was not as difficult a task as it might sound as the whole register was on computer, even so it would take a while to sort out. When Martin rang back, only half an hour later, he gave us the news that one family, the Pullens, had stayed in the hotel a week or so ago but only for one night. Nobody in the hotel could remember them; others might have stayed using a false name but that seemed improbable.

I wondered if it would be possible for me to visit all of the 'take-over families' as I thought of them and then again wondered what I would say to them if I did. On the assumption that one of the families was the guilty one I might just put them on their guard and queer the pitch for the police which perhaps they would not appreciate. I telephoned D.C.I. Plod and, after reminding him who I was, put our theories to him.

I explained that I had used the big university computer to compile a list of the shareholdings of small businesses in which the Jenkins family had within the last few years purchased an interest; I told him that I then went back again using the computer to see who had sold the shares to the Jenkins family. This produced a list of names of people who might have a grudge against Jenkins. I added that I also checked this list of names against the Bull Hotel's register. D.C.I. Blake was on the ball, he had already compared the various lists which he had obtained on his computers, with the hotel register and that he had done this several days ago. He knew about the Pullen family, he told me that the Pullens had a daughter at an expensive boarding school just near Hitchin which was their reason for staying at the hotel periodically. He said there was nothing sinister in that but did agree that any of the take-over families should be considered, he thanked us for our efforts and ask to be kept abreast of any other thoughts we might have.

'I am very happy to listen to any information, ideas or leads that you can provide. Please telephone me if you think of anything else,' he said and rang off. I repeated to Charles all that D.C.I. Blake had said to me.

'He sounds a pretty speedy Plod to me,' said Charles.

❧ CHAPTER 5 ❧

Flatford Mill on a very wet Thursday afternoon may sound dreary but in fact it was enchanting.

I had been wondering how to entertain Charles for the afternoon and then remembered that I had never been to Constable Country, someone suggested it saying that it wasn't so very far away and that even in the rain it might prove interesting. So we went.

We drove from Colchester along the busy A12 to the junction with the B1070, then turned off into East Bergholt and finally in a different world, to Flatford Mill itself. Charles's van just about made it without any incidents although I am far from sure the seats were properly bolted to the floor and I know the contents of the back of the van were not secured in any way at all.

'Is it always as noisy as this?' I asked him.

'It's a bit noisier with the radio on,' he said. 'You may not believe it but I cleaned the van out before I set off this morning, I cleaned it especially for you.'

'It doesn't look like it.'

'You forget it's a working vehicle,' he said. 'It spends it's life going to farms and stables, it bumps along rutted tracks in all weathers getting used and abused. I thought of buying a car but there is nowhere to keep an extra vehicle where I live and I would seldom use it. Vans are always much noisier than cars, there is no carpeting for a start and no rear seats to absorb road and engine noise.'

'It's fine, truly,' I said, wondering why he hadn't at least taken out any of the equine equipment before he started the journey from Hertfordshire. He must have read my thoughts.

'If I take any of my equipment out, for some reason it never all gets put back again. I get to my first appointment to sort out some horse's tooth only to find, half way through a job, that something is missing. I have to drive back to collect it.'

'And all the while the poor horse has its mouth open?'

'I tell you, it really is not the way to impress.'

Perhaps foolishly I put my hand under the seat, I had wanted to adjust the seat a little to give me more leg room, my hand came across an object which on closer inspection, identified itself as a horse's tooth.

'You have spare teeth in here?' I asked

'That's where the horse-tooth fairy lives,' he said giving me a smile. 'Didn't you know there's a horse-tooth fairy'

'Oh yes, and a dog's-tooth fairy too, and a mouse-tooth fairy. Does the mouse still get 6p?'

'I don't know anything about the mouse-tooth fairy, but the horse-tooth fairy gives long life and happiness, to the horse.'

We drove along through the Suffolk countryside, suddenly two great arcs appeared in the sky, magnificent, colourful, the fulfilment of a promise or so the bible would lead us to believe.

'A double rainbow,' we both said at the same time, and laughed.

'Are you going to tell me that's the tooth-fairy's doing?' I asked.

'I rather doubt it actually.'

We stopped the car for the moment, and got out for a better look. There were a few trees in front of us, and the land was fairly flat. The rainbows made a glorious sight.

'It makes me feel as if there is a God after all,' said Charles.

'You're not religious at all then?' I asked.

'Not really no. I always think it is easier to believe in God in the centre of a great cathedral, than in the middle of a car park. I remember Sunday mornings when I was six or seven. My parents pushed me out of the house early on a Sunday morning and sent me off to Sunday School. I think they wanted an hour to themselves in bed but I didn't know that then. I left the house without breakfast or a drink, and ran all the way to the church, I remember it was uphill. When I reached the church it was always a bit cold, I was out of breath, I sat down and felt really strange. A bit faint. I thought it was God entering my body, the holy spirit.'

'What was it?'

'Lack of sugar to the brain I think, I needed sustenance in the form of food and drink rather than the spiritual kind,' said Charles.

'That double rainbow gives food for spiritual thought. Do

you know how they are formed?'

'I know the theory, but it never quite makes sense to me. Double rainbows are caused by a double reflection inside raindrops. I don't know why you sometimes get a double reflection and sometimes you don't and I don't know why the colours are reversed in the second rainbow, but I'm glad it happens and look over there,' said Charles, 'A magic tractor.'

'A what, where?'

'Off to the left, it's turning into a field.'

'Sorry, you've lost me.'

'You have heard of a magician turning a white scarf into a dove?'

'Yes.'

'This is the case of a tractor, turning, into, a, field.' Charles said this very slowly as if talking to a foreign language student.

'Oh very funny.'

We continued our journey, making slow progress through the country lanes but there was no hurry, and no more jokes.

'If you were going to buy a car,' I asked, 'What would it be?'

This is my usual opening gambit with men, it never fails to introduce a sparkle to their eyes, coupled with a happy response, and Charles was no exception, silly bugger. You can do the same thing with women but then its best to ask what they would do if they won the lottery.

'Depends on how much I have to spend,' he said.

'Say £20,000 somewhere around there.'

'Then I would buy a second hand Porsche Boxster.'

'You yuppie!'

'Not really, but I have seen an amazing Boxster for sale with all the extras, as it happens, for just over £20,000, you buy a BMW if you're a yuppie. The Boxster's a dream machine, quite unsuitable for an equine dentist, but great for a business man of substance.'

'Which you are?'

'Which I could be one day if I dream enough,' he said patting his stomach.

'Balderdash,' I said, 'I think a little VW Beetle is nearer your mark.'

'Well what would you get?' asked Charles.

'I wouldn't need £30,000, just £5,000 for a Kawasaki ZX-6R, not that I have been looking,' I added realising that I was as bad as anyone when it comes to dreaming about spending money.

This deep conversation took place at top volume over the rattle and noise created by the van's engine.

'Apart from buying a Boxster, what is your great ambition?' I asked him.

'Apart from buying a Boxster, I should like to play golf really well,' he said.

'I didn't even know you even played. What club do you belong to?'

'I play with friends at their clubs, I have only just got a handicap, it's now 24, so I need practice.'

'How do you get a handicap if you don't belong to a club?'

'I had several lessons with a pro at a pay-as-you-play course and he saw me through. It's a really good game, frustrating, demanding but fantastic when all goes well. I really enjoy it. Have you played?'

'Once, some years ago, I didn't take to it. My problem was that it didn't matter a jot to me whether I got round in 120 or 150 or whatever.'

'I even love watching golf on TV.'

'You are an armchair golfer.'

'Not just an armchair golfer, you must watch TV sometimes.'

'Only neighbours.'

'The soap?'

'The soap.'

'You watch soaps?'

'Afraid so.'

He drove on in silence, it sounded as if I was the first person he had met who enjoyed soaps. Perhaps nobody else admitted it.

'Do you smoke?' I asked after a mile or so of silence. The silence was a relative term, the noise from the van not having diminished.

'No, can't you tell I don't.'

'It's just that there's a funny smell in here, I can't quite place it. I thought it might be something used to hide another smell.'

'Oh yes, I'm sorry about that.'

'But what is it?'

'It's probably horse mouthwash. It seems to pervade the van and me sometimes come to that.'

'So you use it yourself, I suppose it's cheaper than normal mouthwash. I must remember that next time I kiss you, if there is a next time.'

'You haven't complained so far and no I don't use it but I don't expect there is any reason why humans shouldn't, it's probably exactly the same stuff.'

'Accept Charles, accept horse mouthwash?'

'Occupational hazard I fear.'

We drove on finding the car park which was empty, or very nearly so. Almost hiding under an umbrella we first walked to the far side of the river, only wishing we had brought wellingtons; except that I didn't have any. My shoes became muddier and muddier, eventually I cleaned them a bit on some grass and then by standing in a puddle, they were already about as wet as they could get.

The river was so quiet, every time I walk along a river bank, I think of ratty and moley from Wind in the Willows, I suppose many people do. The water was quite still away from the weir, the rain poured down, it was as if we were alone in the world. We walked in Indian file for a mile or so, along the river bank, hardly talking, comfortable in each other's presence. I was trying to identify scenes from Constable's paintings and sketches. Charles walking in front about twice as fast as I could go so I lagged behind a bit.

Retracing our steps we took the pathway to Flatford Mill itself ignoring for the moment the tea room, and the exhibition, but looking carefully at the mill pond and especially carefully at the dry dock which was fascinating. A large hole in the ground very carefully dug out near to the river. The barge would be built at the bottom of the hole, when the construction was finished the sluices were opened releasing river water into the hole, the barge floated away down stream. The painting of this dry dock was in the Tate on loan, last time I visited that gallery, it had caught my eye, both it and the mill are in better condition now than they were when Constable set up his easel, the benefits of tourism.

The mill itself was sitting prettily at the edge of the pond but no wagon was in the water that afternoon.

'Wouldn't you think they would pay someone to sit in a wagon to make the scene authentic?' suggested Charles.

'Perhaps they do in sunny weather.'

We made for the tea shop, Charles selected a boring looking cake which turned out to be gorgeous, so I ordered one too and we sat looking out of the window at the rain pouring onto the water, munching away happily but dripping water everywhere. We were the only ones in the tea room, the shop was empty too save for the attendant from whom I bought an apron with a Victorian workman on the front. The apron was for Charles, I told him it was to encourage housework.

Being wet did really worry us, the amount of water in our hair and clothes was far beyond the capability of the heater in the van to dispel even when it had reached working temperature, we were therefore still sopping wet when we found a car parking space in the middle of Ipswich on the edge of what appeared to be a building site. The rain was bucketing down, we became drenched to the skin the moment we stepped out of the cover of the van notwithstanding our raincoats. Walking along we saw a Turkish restaurant sandwiched between a book shop and an antique shop. We dashed in and found ourselves in a warm dry room with an intriguing smell; but the restaurant was, apart from ourselves, a couple in the corner and a waiter or two, deserted. I particularly dislike eating in empty restaurants but here we were in the dry and we were hungry again, outside it was very wet.

An over-smiling waiter took our raincoats and showed us to a corner table. Charles kindly gave me the seat next to the wall so I had a view of the empty chairs and tables. Almost immediately a waiter came and asked what we would like to drink. Charles because he was driving, refused any alcohol, I hate drinking in the company of someone who is not themselves drinking, we both drank water, as if we had not had enough water that day to last a lifetime. Charles chose Peynirli Sigara Boregi followed by Etli Kuru Fasulye without really knowing what he was ordering and I chose Kuru Fasulye Pilakisi followed by Patlican Firinda, most certainly

I did not know what I was ordering. Even more, we did not know if we were served with the dishes we ordered, but whatever it was, it was very nice indeed.

We were served very round bread rolls by the smiling waiter, unfortunately mine rolled off my side plate when I was nudged, it rolled onto and across the floor. The other couple in the restaurant were just leaving, she, dressed up to the nines, wore high-heeled shoes one of which spiked through my roll. She walked off out of the restaurant with my roll attached to her left shoe thinking no doubt that she looked wonderful, but actually looking a twerp; I didn't like to ask her to return the roll to me.

Half way through, just after our first course, the restaurant seemed to fill up all of a sudden, it filled up with elderly folk, all seemed over sixty. Nothing wrong with that, but we were curious as to why, it was not until we had had our meal and had left the restaurant that we found out there was a special offer for pensioners that day, starting 20 minutes after we went through the door.

When we left the restaurant we were no longer wet or hungry and at last it had almost stopped raining, We walked fairly slowly back to the car, hand in hand, I felt extremely happy.

'That was a good meal, I hardly ever have Turkish food now, I used to at one time,' said Charles.

'Good company too,' I added.

'Do you fancy a walk?'

'Not really, but if you do.'

'No, I have walked enough today, better start back for Colchester then.'

So we did.

'What do you mean, you hardly ever eat Turkish food now? When did you used to?'

'I went to Turkey once,' said Charles, 'Quite a while ago, I went third class by train.'

'That sounds fun.'

'Many amazing and funny things happened. The first was at Canterbury station.'

'Canterbury in Kent.'

'The very same. My ticket was from Waterloo to Istanbul but with the proviso that I could stop off anywhere along route.'

'Yes.'

'So I stopped off at Canterbury on my way down to Dover. I had a girlfriend who, at that time, went to Canterbury University.'

'And you spent a wild hour or so with her.'

'I remember the ticket collector at Canterbury railway station looking at my ticket, looking at me, and saying 'This isn't Istanbul you know.' The poor man thought I had alighted from the train a station or two early.'

'Was she worth breaking your journey for,' I asked not really wanting to know.

'I forget now,' he said tactfully, 'but Istanbul was fantastic, the mosque, the Bosporus, the food, I just liked being there.'

We reached my rooms again having dried off in the restaurant, no longer were we hungry or thirsty. I did put the kettle on but I think both our minds were more on sex. We kissed each other and fairly quickly, partly helping each other, divested coats, tops, shirts, jumpers and jeans. Soon I stood in black lace thong and matching black lace bra. Charles stood in his white Y fronts and black socks; I have to say that I think I was the more glamorous. I made us each a cup of coffee whilst he shed the rest of his exciting garments, returning to find him sitting on one of the college chairs. Putting the coffee down I slipped out of my thong and bra and straddled him so that my legs were either side of him and I was facing him, sitting on his lap. I hoped the chair would support our combined weight, I noticed the full-length mirror on the wardrobe was behind me giving Charles an excellent view of my rear. Charles was very erect, he rubbed against my pubic hair. We kissed, he massaged my breasts, I lightly fingered him running my thumb and index finger up over and around him. After only a few seconds or so I raised myself up and forwards settling on top of him, wriggled a little so he entered me and penetrated me as far as possible. His hands moved from my nipples to my bum and stroked me continuously, I wriggled a little more but I had no intention, our love-making being over in the space of just a few moments by causing anything to happen prematurely.

Getting off him, I ask him to lie down on my bed on his

back. Then I sat astride him facing away from him with my bottom about three inches from his face, pinning his arms by the sides of his body with my knees. I wasn't sure if he liked oral sex, and didn't want to put the question to him in so many words. The way I positioned my body, if he wanted to, he could, if he chose to nibble me by raising his head off the pillow; or if he did not choose he had a grand view of my naked bottom bobbing around. I bent forwards and licked him, and then took him in my mouth, realising that he did indeed like oral sex, his tongue flicked in and out of me delightfully. I should have liked to say that my breasts dangled against him but they were far too small for such an adventure. Fearful that he was becoming too excited again after not too long, I crumpled onto the floor, lying on my back to see what he would do.

He did not disappoint, he bent my knees so they touched my breasts, then taking his weight on his arms placed either side of my shoulders he leaned his body against me his chest laying on my knees, his stomach against my shins. Slowly he entered me a little, then more and more until the whole length of his shaft was inside me. Then he rocked backwards and forwards hardly moving at first then with more and more energy all the time looking into my eyes. We climaxed together and I hate to say so but a little noisily.

❧ CHAPTER 6 ❧

On my return to my rooms this time alone, as Charles had had to get back for an early start in the morning, I found a note for me pushed under the door. Not all of the college rooms were yet equipped with telephones and mine, one of the older ones, was one of the ones without this facility; any important message had to be relayed by one of the porters, who would walk round with the message. If one received too many messages one's popularity with the porters was in danger of declining. This particular message read "Urgent, telephone D.C.I. Blake first thing in the morning," and as an after thought. "Please telephone him before 9 o'clock."

My room, indeed the building itself felt a bit empty, lonely all of a sudden but the note helped me get back to reality. I wondered what the police could possibly want with me again. Mechanically I took my clothes off, cleaned my teeth, cleaned me, got into bed, put the light out and did not go to sleep. Usually I am asleep within a few moments of my head touching the pillow but not that night; my mind was too active, I started worrying about having made a fool of myself in front of Charles, that my masters course was too difficult for me, that I had no real friends, that the hotel would go bust, my bike would crash. My method of dealing with these imponderables is to have to hand in my memory a list of small but important successes as a counterweight to the negative thoughts. This usually succeeds. Grades for my last piece of work were not at all bad, the hotel made a bit of a profit during the last twelve months, the ride down to Colchester had been a dream and I had been driving the bike very carefully. Charles seemed to like me, all positive thoughts which made not an h'appeth of difference to my ability to sleep. Heaving myself up on one elbow I turned to Shakespeare and re-read sonnet XXIX, and then re-read a chapter from 'The Situation in Flushing' by Edmund Lowe. This gives the story of the childhood of a boy from the village of Flushing in Michigan. He was born at the beginning of the last century, about 1903, it is a good yarn, amusing, happy, fascinating if you are fond of steam engines, not that I am, or social history which is much nearer my mark.

Suddenly I woke up, it was morning, my reading had done the trick, I must have dozed off, it was now 8.50 am, my first lecture was not until 11 o'clock so there was no hurry, I relaxed back into the pillows and I thought, half awake and half asleep, of the events of the day before, mulling them over in my mind. At least, there was no hurry until I spotted the slip of paper lying on top of the pile of unread history books, suddenly there was some urgency after all, I had a telephone call to make, to D.C.I. Plod who obviously worked far longer hours than I did.

In the event I could not get through to D.C.I. Blake on the telephone, perhaps he also was having a lie in that morning. I did reach his pretty assistant whose name did not stick,

Police Constable Mercy it sounded like but I don't think it was.

'Good morning Miss Wright,' said Pretty Assistant, 'Thank you for ringing. D.C.I. Blake wants to stage a reconstruction of the crime. He would have liked to have done it yesterday, exactly a week after the murder had taken place but it proved impossible for a variety of reasons. Mr Martin Lynch your manager, tells us that there are no functions booked in at the Bull Hotel this evening, the hotel is only half full and everybody is available, so the intention is to hold the reconstruction during this afternoon and evening. Would you please return to Hitchin as soon as you can and in any event before 2 o'clock today.'

'Yes of course I will. I have a lecture at 11 o'clock, it's for one hour, I should be back at the Bull Hotel by 1.30, would that be acceptable?'

It was and she rang off. I didn't like the sound of the hotel being only half full, perhaps it was time I popped back. To save time I thought it wise to wear my bike leathers to the lecture hall, in fact they are not made of leather at all but of a special new material, kevlar I think it's called. Everyone always teases me when I appear with crash helmet under my arm, dressed in black and silver, they call me bovver girl and the biker. I smiled happily and took a place near the door for an easy exit.

The lecture did overrun, so I slipped out a bit early, at noon, walked to my bike, it started first go as it always did and off I rode through the car park, along a narrow country lane to the main Clacton Road, over the double roundabout, through Colchester, and out onto the open road, the A12. The bike's great engine humming under me, cruising at around 5500 revs, wonderful freedom, I headed for home, except I am never quite sure where home is. The hotel never seems like a home, I can't cook there, or wash my laundry. I cannot have a real party, nor ever have a row, I must always be on my best behaviour, that is not what I would call home: yet my rooms in college are not home either. I cannot paint the walls, or personalise them; perhaps they are all home. I remember a walking holiday in the Lake District with some friends years back. We were camping, carrying everything on our backs, there were three of us. We had walked from Langdale to the Great Gable by way of Mickelden and Angel Tarn onto Sty Head and then down to Ennerdale. The plan was to walk to the near end of Ennerdale Water then to retrace our steps back to a chosen campsite where the ground was a little more level than it was in other parts and there were not quite as many rocks and stones lying on the ground.

Our load was very heavy so we left our rucksacks under a copse of trees whilst we trudged the three miles or so down to the water's edge and the arduous three miles or so back again. Coming back it was gloomy walking between the conifers, we were very tired indeed and hungry too, we had misjudged quite how far it was and I longed to get home, which in that instant, was a bundle of plastic and metal containing some protein and carbohydrate in the shape of a filled ruck sack. Home must be where your stomach is.

I reached Hitchin almost on the dot of 1.30 pm. One of the difficulties of riding a bike is the lack of available time pieces, it is very difficult to glance at your watch when your arm is covered in many layers of clothing, so timing is usually a matter of guesswork, yet it is a little easier to keep to schedules than it is when driving a car as roadworks and traffic jams do not present the same difficulties; speed limits don't change though.

On entering the Bull I was met by D.C.I. Blake himself, he was standing in the middle of the Bull Hotel lounge, an intimidating figure, no wonder he was alone. Just at that moment Pretty Assistant walked in, it was she who asked me to go to wherever I was at 1.30 the previous Thursday and there make a schedule of my movements during the rest of that afternoon and evening; then repeat whatever that was so I would be retracing my steps of eight days ago. I knew that just before 2 pm on that Thursday afternoon I was listening to Rosemary in the churchyard shopping area, so I returned there and wrote out the schedule of my activities for that afternoon and evening as Pretty Assistant had requested. A little easier said than done, for who looks at their watch every ten or fifteen minutes. I knew where I was to start with and knew the time of my interview with the engaged couple, but I was far from certain what I was doing for the whole of the rest of the day. I don't recall doing very much except supervising things generally.

Nevertheless the time of my appointment with the young couple seeking a wedding venue was fixed, so after a few moments I walked rather than hurried back to the hotel, smiled at Gloria who was on the telephone in reception and went up to my room. I showered, thinking that I needed a shower anyway, changed and walked downstairs, nodding to Ian and Gloria entering the hotel lounge. I then realised that I should have spoken to Gloria and Ian and did not know whether to go back or not. A constable was sitting in the lounge and told me to keep on going.

The couple were not present, so I had to show myself around my hotel which seemed odd and said goodbye to the empty space where they would have stood. I carried on with my routine crossing the path of members of my staff as they were in the process of carrying out their own schedule.

D.C.I. Plod called me over at one time and asked me how things were going and whether anything had struck me as being strange or out of place. We talked for a few minutes, he was obviously keeping an eye on everything and staying in touch with everyone.

'Would you consider everything you have seen today Miss White,' he said. 'I'll want to talk to you again, would you be free tomorrow evening at say, 6 o'clock please. I will meet you here at the Bull Hotel if I may. Now continue with the reconstruction doing the best you can.'

So I went on my way.

I met people who had not been where they were, that is according to my memory and didn't meet people who I should have met but we did our best. All went fairly smoothly as far as I could see, until about 9 o'clock, then part of my world fell apart and it had nothing to do with D.C.I. Blake or the death of Richard Jenkins.

I found myself standing in the reception area next to Martin, both of us were at something of a loose end. I try to show an interest in what my friends or employees are enthusiastic about and I remembered that Martin had returned from his holiday in France enthusing about the new wines he had found. At the time I had almost cut him dead and this was a good moment to make amends.

'Martin,' I said, 'Tell me about this wine that you brought back from France. Is it really that good, or was it really good in the French countryside but loses something on the journey home.'

'Lucy,' he said, 'You be the judge. Let the pair of us slip down into the cellars, with a couple of glasses and we will have an impromptu wine-tasting session.'

'Well yes,' I agreed, 'But I am not very good at spitting it out.'

'Just a couple of glasses then, for professional purposes,' and he led me through an ancient door set in the wall, almost unnoticeable, walked down some old steps and reached the cellars which were huge, stretching as they did, under the whole of the old part of the building. In so far as I was aware, the cellars had never been decorated, they must have looked very much as they look today, for the last two hundred years at least. There were cobwebs, only to be expected, it was dusty but not dirty and it was very orderly. In the far corner was a ramp for bringing the drink into the hotel from the lorry, usually the drink came in the form of crates and barrels. A bottle lift was used to raise liquor up to the bars, various tubes and cylinders appeared to be part of the order of things as did barrels, casks and along part of one wall, stretching into the middle of the cellar were racks of wine. There seemed to be hundreds of them far more than I remembered.

'I'd forgotten how long it has been since I have been down here, it must be two or three years. I used to play down here as a child,' I said. 'We seem to have a great deal of wine in store.'

'There are 4,862 bottles down here, or were before I went away on holiday, I haven't done a stock-take since I have been back, but we often sell 400 or 500 bottles a week, so we have only nine or ten weeks supply, not very much really, in fact not enough. Naturally some of the more expensive wine is slow to shift and might be left on the shelves for some months, whereas the cheaper bottles would probably be sold within a month.'

'And where is this fabulous wine you mentioned?'

'It's over here but I didn't say it was fabulous, it isn't, not at that price, mind you it does taste very good indeed, it is reasonably priced, and fills a gap in our wine list. Look, I have two glasses, first of all let's try this bottle of claret, Chateau-Grand-Puy-Lacoste. Very deftly indeed Martin uncorked the bottle of French wine and poured out a little in the two glasses both of which he held in one hand. He did the whole process so quickly and professionally that one could not help being impressed.

Martin started chatting about wine, using words like full bodied, leaving a pleasant aftertaste, could I detect the hint of blackberry he went on about its nose. To my great shame it just tasted of a most pleasant wine to me. He talked on, telling me of the wine he enjoyed, the places he had visited, and the people he had met especially one couple who treated him as an honoured guest. Proudly they produced wine from years past set aside for a special occasion and opened it once they realised Martin's expertise. His enthusiasm was infectious and I enjoyed the half hour I spent with him, we walked around the racks, he explained about this one and that one, how one was meant to be kept a little longer. He showed me clarets and reds from California and Argentina, moving along the shelving from one batch to another. Then we heard voices above our heads.

'There is no ceiling to the cellars,' said Martin, 'You can always hear what is being said in the room above. That must be one of the waitresses in the linen storeroom chatting. It sounds like Sharon to me.'

It was Sharon, but Sharon was talking to Charles, and it sounded to me as if he was chatting her up. I knew Charles was proposing to call for me, but I didn't know he knew Sharon, and I did not know he wanted to know Sharon rather better. I could hear every word the rotten sod was saying. 'You'll come round to my house later on then, I look forward so much to seeing you.'

And I thought we were an item. I thought Charles wanted me, I had heard quite enough, I was furious, I marched up the stairs, walked to the linen cupboard and threw my glass of wine at him and then march off.

I don't know what he did, I didn't care any more, hell, I thought, I hate being hurt. I went up to my room feeling really lonely. To block the world out I put on my headphones and listened to a Beethoven Symphony, his third. I thought Charles might come up to my room and I didn't want to hear his excuses. After a little while I realised I should organise something to do for the next day, Saturday, otherwise I would just mope. First I telephoned Caroline to see if by any chance a horse might be available to ride and by a happy chance there was. A small group had hired a mini cross country course and invited me to join them. That should take care of the morning. Charles came a knocking at my door again, I told him to go away, or words to that effect. I thought I might go shopping in the afternoon and see some friends in the evening after I had had my session with the police. Perhaps I could arrange a girlie night out. I was in the mood for that, I thought.

Having lived in Hitchin all of my life, I knew scores of

people, especially girls of my own age, some I knew well and some were really only acquaintances. I started telephoning a number of girl friends and in about an hour had arranged my evening. As it happened, it turned out to be a night in for me, as I agreed to host the do in the lounge of the Bull. It took me an hour or so to arrange, for everyone I telephoned wanted to chat, there's a surprise.

I lay on my bed, desperate not to feel sorry for myself. In the end I decided to carry out a final tour of the hotel before turning in for the night and on my round bumped into Gillian.

'Hello Miss White, I'm afraid I'm all behind,' she said, 'The police kept asking me questions, which I suppose is inevitable but it does take up a great deal of time.'

'What did they ask you?' I enquired.

'Questions about you, had I seen Jenkins previously, describe the objects lying around in Room 26 when I went in that evening, as if I could. I just went in and did my job and came out again. If you go into hotel rooms every night one after another to turn the bed down, the only thing that strikes one is anything strange, not if it was the same as the night before.'

'Could anyone have borrowed your uniform?'

'Not with me wearing it, I suppose after I left for the evening they could, it was locked up in my locker. By the by, I don't think guests ever actually look at me as a person, rather they look at me as a chambermaid. They just see the uniform.'

'The police seem to think,' I said, 'that someone, probably female, bought a bottle of spiked wine, two glasses and two biscuits on a tray and left them there by Jenkin's bedside. Then when Jenkins returned to his room, he had a drink of the wine, was poisoned and died.'

'I didn't poison him,' said Gillian, 'I didn't even know him.'

'No one is suggesting you did, but you might have seen something.'

'Well truly I didn't.'

'I, and The police need to establish how the person delivered the tray into the bedroom after spiking the wine. How they got hold of the biscuits, the glasses, the tray, and the uniform if they wore a uniform.'

'Why do you think they wore a uniform?'

'Because it would look very strange if someone who was not dressed in the correct garb, started to carry out room service. It would be noticeable.'

'Yes I do see the point you're making but I simply don't think I can help you and heavens is that the time, I really must go I am late already. Lucy, if you are about, I will drop in tomorrow or at least give you a ring and we can chat then if you want to, although I really don't think I can add anything to what I have already said. I must have said it all four times now, you take care, goodnight,' and with that, she slipped off.

I continued my tour around the hotel, quietly,

unobtrusively, my intention was not to catch my staff out, rather to give them any assurance or backup they needed. Often all I did was to pick up bits of litter that guests had inadvertently dropped. The bars were still fairly full, I stopped to serve a group and then a couple who wanted a bit of a chat. I collected empty glasses off tables putting them on a side counter ready to be washed up and polished. The washing is easy, just hold the glass against a electrically turning brush and leave to dry, the polishing takes a little time and is done in the quieter moments if there are any. The bar serves snacks and coffee as well as drinks and packets of crisps. Patrons help themselves to cutlery which is pre wrapped in a paper napkin. The cutlery is on a table near the bar, next to coffee cups, individual non-dairy creamers, and individual biscuits. It was as plain as a pikestaff that anyone who wished to, could obtain a packet or two of the hotel biscuits without notice or comment. They were there for the taking.

The trays too were easy to come by, indeed anyone who ordered a round of more than two drinks was automatically offered a tray by the bar staff to enable them to take the drinks safely away from the bar to their table.

Alistair Gentle was my barman, he had a passion for real ale every bit as intense as Martin's passion for wine, yet the two men hardly got on together. They seldom spoke except for strictly business concerns. Martin being hotel manager was theoretically in charge of everything so Alistair was under him but that hardly applied in practice. Apart from making sure staffing levels were acceptable and no under-age drinking took place Martin's involvement in the bars was to collect up the money and balance the books. Alistair did the ordering, chose the snack menus, served patrons, trained junior staff, he would not have taken kindly at all to any suggestions put forward by Martin. Alistair did tolerate me but I suspect only as far as he had to. We had always got on reasonably well, he had worked first as my parent's employee, then as mine. My change in status still gave him a little trouble, it was not something which was easily absorbed by him.

'How goes it Alistair?' I asked as we bumped against each other, both of us reaching for the mixers shelves.

'It has been a good night tonight,' he said. 'Friday night usually sees several groups of men enjoying their beer in the public bar, with mixed and ladies groups in the saloon and tonight was no exception. This is becoming a very popular drinking place with several sections of the community, we have been very busy, there's a lot of money in that till for you.'

Martin and I had developed a system that whenever the till itself was getting too full of money, some of the contents would be pushed into the top of a cash box, the box was bolted to the floor under the counter. It wasn't a proper safe, probably anyone could break into it with a heavy hammer but it was a great deal safer than the till which was continuously opened and was within easy reach of the counter top. We never kept money in the cash box over night. The system allowed bar staff to reduce the notes in the till without leaving the bar area. Once an evening, more often at, for example, Christmas, usually after the last of the drinks had been served the box was emptied into a colour-coded plastic bag with the date written on a paper tag attached to the bag and then that plastic bag was dropped into the hotel safe.

Each of the four departments within the hotel which took money, namely the bar, the reception desk, the function room and the restaurant had the same system only with differing coloured plastic bags. I took a handful of notes from the till, and slipped them into the cash box leaving ample £5 and £10 in case a rush of £20 appeared.

'Alistair, I think you're a wonderful barman, you have made the place have a great atmosphere, no wonder we are always busy. Incidentally do you think people pinch the biscuits we put out?' I asked.

'I wouldn't be a bit surprised,' he said, 'but I take the view that they only cost a few pence, the goodwill value is there, and I suspect we sell more beer if people can have a nibble. If it worries you, we could put a price ticket on them. How about ten pence, just about enough to cover the cost.'

'I leave it to you,' I said. 'If you want to try it, do. Has anyone been talking about the murder?'

'Just about everyone, it has increased trade enormously.'

'Good heavens, I should have thought people would have stayed away but I suppose they're curious. Did you know Jenkins, that's the man who died?'

'I must have met him, but I don't remember him specifically, the police asked me the same question; they also asked me if anyone starts fights here, I don't see how that relates to anything.'

This conversation was carried out in fits and starts between serving customers, dealing with glasses and coffee cups, we snatched words together as we were able to.

'Yes, well that was my next question, the theory goes that Jenkins was going to get his thugs to start fights in the hotel to drive clients away so I would be forced to sell. Have you had any fights here at all in the last week or two?'

'As I told the police, we have not had any fights in the bar since just before Christmas, and that was Eddy Weaver causing problems, nothing unusual there.'

I gave him a half smile, I was still really upset inside.

'Is Eddy Weaver still with us, I haven't seen him for a very long time; he used to sit me on his lap when I was tiny, he used to tell me stories.'

Martin walked into the bar. He, being the manager on duty was responsible for the whole hotel and having the police around, didn't make his job any easier. Martin had come to empty the cash box which had been collecting money all evening, and to keep an eye on things in general. When he saw me he smiled.

'I heard there was a bit of a tiff,' he said.

'I broke one of my cardinal rules,' I said, 'I wasn't on duty, but I still should not have lost my temper in public. Where is the rotten man, I have been trying to avoid him'

'I believe he has slipped off now but I didn't see him go.'

Alistair was serving another customer, I walked off with Martin after he had collected the notes from the cash box.

'That tasted excellent wine to me,' I said, 'If you still think it is as good as you say, do import some more.'

'I thought you had forgotten about it.'

'No, just the reverse, I smelt it, sipped it and then poured it away, it is just that someone got in the way when I was pouring it away.'

'Perhaps it is a good job that he did get in the way, you chose the laundry cupboard so it's quite lucky that all of the white napkins are not covered in red wine stains. As it happens I hadn't yet got to opening the bottle I was talking about, I was working up to it.'

'I wondered if you would like to start a sort of mini wine society.' I said changing the subject speedily, 'it has to be entirely up to you but I think you would enjoy it. You could hold monthly meetings in the hotel, produce the wine for tasting, take a small subscription to cover the cost and perhaps sell some of the wine by the caseload. The hotel would charge for the meal, the hotel would import the wine and make a profit and there would be a bonus in it for you.'

'It is certainly a thought,' said Martin.

'Think about it,' I said.

We wandered along to reception together still holding the plastic bag full of takings from the bars which he deposited in the big hotel safe where it would be secure until the banks opened again. We then made our way to the dining room continuing a tour of inspection. There, in the dining room were a party of about eleven people who had come late to dine, calling on spec; they were in the middle of eating their dessert all of them having chosen a slice of raspberry pavlova to finish off their meal. Apart from that group, an elderly couple in the far corner were lingering over empty coffee cups, gazing at each other but hardly talking, they looked rather upset to me. A noisy party of four, none of whom could have been over the age of 22 years, were ordering more wine having finished their meals long since. Nothing strange or unusual in the dining room, everything was nicely under control, apart from my emotions, considerably unhappy I took myself off to bed.

✤ CHAPTER 7 ✤

Saturday morning; a dull day, not sunny, not raining, not blustery, it matched my mood. I felt weary but made myself get up and go for a jog. I ran quite quickly as far as Charlston, a pretty hamlet with a delightful pub, not that I was thinking of entering the hostelry as part of my exercise routine. I crossed the tiny bridge over the stream at the side of the pub, ran up through a copse, along a bridle path eventually ending up in Gosmore before turning back towards the centre of Hitchin and the Bull. Hot, sweaty, exhausted I showered, changed and went down to breakfast reading a newspaper at the table as was my habit. I felt relaxed for the first time for 12 hours. Breakfast was only museli toast with coffee and juice but I lingered over it for quite a time.

Walking through reception on my way out of the dining room Ian called me over. He was on duty that morning, his last morning at the hotel under the work experience scheme although I had decided to have a talk with him about either staying on or returning when he was able to do so.

'Miss White,' he said, 'I need some help please.' He was holding a letter in his hand and at the same time peering over the computer screen looking perplexed.

'We have had a letter from a guest who says we have over charged him. He says he stayed for one night only, but that we had charged him for several days. I have checked the computer and he definitely stayed from Thursday to Sunday

114

afternoon, where do I go from here?'

I walked over to where he was sitting and stood behind his chair, looking over his shoulder.

'You have him down as being in Room 26 but that's the room Jenkins was murdered in, who is the letter from?'

'Mr Jeff Barrett, he was in Room 16, I remember I muddled up, Gloria helped me put the records in order. We went through it all carefully together and she showed me what to do.'

'If you remember Ian, you were under considerable stress because of what Jenkins had done to your father. You told me that he had made your father sell his business at an under value. Let me have a proper look.'

I gently eased him from the chair in front of the computer screen and I sat down in his place.

'The amendments you and Gloria made are all here but they have not been activated. They are still being held in this sub file. I don't know why Gloria did it like that, why she didn't just change it.'

'I was doing it with Gloria looking over my shoulder, I thought it best to get it quite correct, so saved it to a sub file first, I checked it through, then I thought I brought it onto the main programme and saved it.'

'Well it didn't make it onto the main programme. Best to send Mr Barrett a refund and an apology. If anyone wants me, I am not here. I am off riding,' I said and made for the door.

'Just a minute, please, tell me what to say to him.'

I dictated a letter for Ian to send to Jeffrey Barrett, enclosing a cheque for the sum overpaid, I dictated it slowly so that Ian could write it down and be able to read it again, I asked him if he was happy with it. He said he was so I left him to it and made for the car park.

When I drove up to the stables, in Todds Green, they were deserted, only a note left under an old horse shoe told me that the cross country had to be postponed. That was fine, I could still ride. I brought Archie from his stable, tied him to the wall using the special slip knot, groomed him carefully, cleaned out his hooves, brushed his tail and put a saddle and bridle on him remembering to put on his martingale before his saddle, usually I forgot and had to redo the girth. I collected my hat and stick, brought Archie to the mounting block and once on his broad back walked him up the lane. As soon as possible I pushed him into trot and tried to make sure that my hands were as still as possible, my heels were lower than my toes, in other words that I rode properly. Once out into the open countryside we had a slow canter, and then, when the way was clear, a full gallop. I wasn't bothered about the scenery that day, I needed exhilaration and got it. We galloped in an enormous circle over land set aside under the E.U. farm policy. We trotted then finally walked back to the stables. As always my mood had changed, I felt that the affairs in Hitchin were not nearly as significant to me as they seemed an hour or so before. I cleaned Archie down, gave him a thank you stroke, a few nuts and a carrot and led him to the meadow to spend the rest of the day grazing. There can be fewer more peaceful sights than watching horses graze. To earn my keep I returned to the tack room and cleaned and oiled both bridle and saddle and swept up the yard. I left still without seeing anyone.

It would have been really good to have chatted over my problems with someone and I tried to telephone my Uncle George two or three times, he had been in the local police force for over twenty years, ending up as an Inspector. His shoulder would have been a welcome support but there was no reply to my call. He and my aunt were probably in France visiting their town house near La Rochelle. If they were over there they were out of contact, I didn't know the number and wasn't quite sure of the full address.

I had hardly put the receiver down after my third try to call my uncle when Anna telephoned me. She was one of the friends who was going to join me for supper that evening and I thought at first she was ringing to say she couldn't come after all; on the contrary, she suggested we went on a shopping trip. She needed to buy some clothes and would I join her.

'That would be great,' I said. 'When are you leaving?'

'In about half an hour, I'll pick you up.'

Anna is never on time but it didn't really matter. She drove up in her mini ages after she said she would arrive, and tooted her horn; I jumped in and we were away. Anna is not the best of drivers, she tends to look at the person she's talking to so her steering becomes erratic. I do the same thing a bit but I think I drive a straighter line. She also keeps being bumped from behind at roundabouts. It's quite alarming and it's because she changes her mind as to whether to wait for a particular car or go before the car reaches her; nevertheless unscathed we reached destination, Welwyn, where there is a large store. Anna said that she was after something to wear that evening.

'But it's only an informal get together,' I explained.

'If you believe that, you're crazy,' she said. 'This is one occasion where everyone will be making an impression. What are you going to wear?'

'I thought grey slacks and a red sweater, although I have had them both for a couple of years or more.'

'Then they won't do at all. Looks like we are shopping for two.'

We parked up and were making our way to the centre when I was stopped by a middle aged couple both laden down with their bags.

'Aren't you Lucy White?' I was asked.

'Yes, do I know you?'

'We are Ian's parents. Ian who has been working for you at the Bull.'

'Oh yes, we haven't met, I am pleased to see you. Ian has been doing really well.'

'We stopped you because we wanted to say how glad we are that Richard Jenkins has died. Well done, well done indeed. We will give you all our support.' And with that, they walked off.

'What was that all about?' asked Anna.

'I think they think I'm a murderess,' I explained. 'Does that prove that Ian's family is not involved?'

'I lead such a humdrum life compared with you. I can't envisage anyone ever coming up to me and saying that.'

'Nor could I a month ago.'

'Why do they think it was you?'

'The police seem to think it was an inside job. I had opportunity, I had motive and no alibi, the fact that I didn't do it is a mere detail.'

The shopping was a success, not only because we both bought outfits to wear but also because we talked and talked. I returned ready to face the world again.

At 6 o'clock I duly presented myself to D.C.I. Blake. I was nervous, no doubt it showed.

'There you are,' he said smiling, trying to put me at my ease. 'I thought perhaps a chat might be helpful.'

'A chat?'

'Just a chat, come and sit down. When I interview you formally, which I will have to do in due course, I won't be able to ask you your view on things in quite the same way and there are likely to be other people present and that tends to dilute discussion. Just for the moment, let's just have a chat.

My colleagues and I are still analysing yesterday's reconstruction, did anything else occur to you, however small or insignificant?'

'No, not really, except people were not where I expected them to be some of the time.'

'Yes that is almost inevitable, bearing in mind that nobody actually keeps a check on what time he or she does things during the day unless they have a particular appointment. I have to say that nothing exceptional shows out of the reenactment, except that your guests in Room 14 are certain that they saw a chambermaid walking up the stairs with a tray of drinks, sometime soon after 9 o'clock. Now we do not think it was Gillian as she was doing one of the other floors at that time. We are left with alternatives, these are that Room 14 is mistaken as to the time, that they are mistaken altogether and did not see a chambermaid, Gillian is mistaken as to the time and it was her, or it could be someone else. We must not assume that the person carrying that tray was the murderer or murderess but it is thought provoking.'

'Cannot the people in Room 14 describe the person they saw?' I asked.

'Not really but they did their best. Ordinary looking, they said, with hair tied back. About five foot six inches, medium build, female, wearing a uniform, it doesn't help a great deal, the description could fit almost any one of your chambermaids. We have checked and find that anyone can obtain the wine of the type used from several local stores, the biscuits are freely available from your bar, the tray and glasses likewise from the bar but the key and the uniform are more difficult and that is where I would like your help, hence this chat.'

'I will help all I can.' I said.

'Of course you will. Let's discuss the key. Are you aware that many of your room keys are pass keys?'

'Pass keys?'

'In most hotels, each room has its own individual key and the management have a number of pass keys that fit all of the locks or all of the locks on a particular floor so that chambermaids and the like can gain access to the room when the guests are absent.'

'Yes I know what a pass key is, I have my own.'

'Of course you do but what I am saying is that, well let's take an example. The key to Room 32 appears to fit all of the locks in the hotel. Room 32's key, the one you give to guests staying in Room 32, is actually a pass key for the whole hotel. Many of the room keys are also pass keys but not all of them, but no one would usually know that. One or two of the older chambermaids know it but an outsider wouldn't. You are saying that even you did not know it.'

'Really I didn't know that, I'm speechless, I will have to get new locks fitted or new keys cut.'

'To gain entry without Mr Jenkin's knowledge, the phantom chambermaid would either have to have copied the pass key, borrowed a pass key or used one of the keys which doubled as a pass key. All to my mind would require inside knowledge.'

'Perhaps the wine was delivered to Mr Jenkins whilst he was in his room, he could have opened the door himself, then no key would be required.' I said.

'We have thought of that, but have largely discounted the idea. If you murder someone, you will know the victim well unless you are a hired killer and no hired killer would use poison in this manner. It would be extraordinary if it were not so, except for people of celebrity status. If you know the victim it more or less supposes that the victim knows you. Outside domestic situations, in other words where a wife is trying to kill her husband, it would be very odd for the murderer to knock on the victims door and say, "Here is a bottle of wine you did not order, yes I know you know me, you know I don't like you but please drink the wine," it doesn't work.'

'Yes, that's right. I follow your reasoning.' I said feeling like Watson to his Holmes.

'The wine has to appear to be a complimentary bottle from the hotel management, so the question of the pass key is still very much alive. Let's now turn to the uniform. Spare uniforms are kept on the third floor,' said D.C.I. Blake.

'Yes, that's right.'

'In fact, they are in a wardrobe off a store cupboard, on the third floor. Only someone associated with the hotel, or who has stayed in the hotel as a guest and done some exploring, would know where the uniforms are kept. It would be very strange for a guest to ask a member of staff where they keep spare uniforms and if anyone did ask a question like that, it would be remembered.'

'Yes, I still follow your reasoning.'

'You and Ian Witty are both associated with the hotel, both had a motive and both had opportunities, you both had pass keys and both knew where the uniforms were kept. I am telling you all this because I am fairly sure you did not kill him. You only had a motive if you knew what Mr Jenkins was planning and I do not think he had told you yet. He had yet to make any overtures to you but I could be wrong. Yet the keys and the uniform point to an inside job, we have tried to work out how many uniforms there are but even that has been difficult. Each female member of your permanent staff is issued with two uniforms, one to wear and one to wash. Everyone still has their quota in their possession. You issue temporary female staff with a uniform at the beginning of each shift and the chambermaid in charge of these uniforms has no real idea as to how many spare sets there are. She never counts them, she thinks there are about nine of them but it could just as easily be eight or ten. How many do you think you have?'

'I have no idea at all, there are always some being laundered, some in for repair, it is the nature of things but there seems to be enough.'

123

'Yes there is enough, more than enough, because you have several different sizes. There is no point giving a size ten to a size sixteen person.'

'Or vice versa.'

'Quite, in fact you have seventeen chambermaid dresses, excluding the dresses issued to permanent staff, and twenty four aprons. You also have twenty three hats but few of the chambermaids wear hats nowadays, although one or two of them do if for example their hair needs cutting.'

'You have been busy.'

'We have been diligent, yes.'

'But where is all this leading us?' I asked.

'Bear with me. I am really just thinking aloud. No casual thief would just happen across a spare uniform locked away in a wardrobe off a store room on the third floor. It is impossible to visualise an outsider walking up those three flights, going into the stockroom and then the wardrobe, taking out the uniform just on the off chance. So either the murderess is versed in the intimate ways of the hotel or the guests in Room 14 were mistaken. Can you add anything to this?'

'You seem to be implying that it was me who committed the crime?'

'Not at all. It might be a friend of someone who works here, who asked casually where the uniforms are kept. There is no reason why it is a secret. It might be a guest who made the enquiry some time ago, there is still much work to be done. Take Ian, he might have mentioned the facts of the key and the uniform when chatting to one of his female relatives.'

'I am sure it wasn't Ian.'

'How long have you known him, is it ten days or so. Anyway he might not even have realised that he told them vital information and I am not saying it was Ian, I'm just having a friendly chat with you.'

'What about the poison; poison isn't easy to come by, doesn't that lead you somewhere?'

'Obviously we are looking into that but I don't want to make anything public yet. The experts are suggesting that there was more than one type of poison used and that complicates matters enormously. It seems that in all of the text books, the reaction of a particular poison is explained. For example, if you take arsenic, everyone knows what the symptoms are, if you take strychnine other symptoms will show but what if you mix the two together with a third, what are the symptoms then? The text books I have read don't help and we're starting from the other direction, we don't know which poisons were used, but as I say, there seems to be more than one, perhaps several mixed together. As you see it is complicated. We will get there in the end but it may take a little while. That, as they say, is my problem but if you think of anything else, please contact me straight away.'

'Of course I will, I am really anxious for the matter to be cleared up,' and with that I left.

The girlie night, in to me, out to them, went very well. We

took over the lounge at the Bull, ate a simple meal of chicken noodle soup, crusty bread, lamb chops and salad with Jersey Royal potatoes which had been bought in the spring, part boiled and frozen. We ended with fruit salad, no cream. Everyone, or very nearly everyone had asked for a diet friendly meal and this is what was served. We had all known each other for many years, most of us had been at Hitchin Girls School together and there was much chatting, bringing each other up to date with husbands, lovers, children, holidays, jobs or lack of them.

I think we all talked at once for most of the evening. I remember Mary telling me:

'I've just met Ben, he telephones at least once a day. I think he might be the one.'

At the same time as Emily said to me:

'With Eurostar shopping in France is so easy, we go four or five times a year.'

Whilst Heather was saying to Emily:

'No no, London is the place to shop, unless you can get as far as Paris.'

We all wanted to try on Judy's new ring and the chatter got louder and louder but silence suddenly reigned when we heard Mary say 'the problems my husband had with my crutchless knickers, has anyone found them to be really satisfactory? He got a bit stuck when ... well just when really.'

We all laughed. Judy then broke in by telling us about her holiday in Cornwall. 'On one occasion I went to the beach and watched a middle aged lady change into a swimming costume under a bit too small towel. She was trying to put on a one-piece bathing suit but inadvertently, under the towelling, put her legs into the costume the wrong way round, so it was on back to front. When the time came to pull up the top bit over her boobs, it was not there. The top part of her costume I mean, her boobs were still there. Obviously the top half of her costume was hanging down behind her back. Everyone realised this including her husband, the poor lady kept saying, "I know this isn't a bikini". Her husband told her that her top part was behind her, as it was. The lady turned round and of course the top half of her costume turned round with her. Her husband had a fit of the giggles and couldn't get a word out. She took it all in very good spirits. Even the lifeguards smiled.'

It was a good evening, lasting until 11 o'clockish when they left and I went to bed having partaken of my fair share of the alcohol.

Sometime in the small hours I was awakened from a deep sleep. I could hear ringing. At first I thought it must be the church bells from St Mary's, but it wasn't sounding right, it was dreadful, going on and on. I lay for a few moments trying to work out what could be making that noise, before I realised that it was the fire alarm, the hotel was on fire.

I leapt out of bed and rushed for the door and opened it before I realised that I was still naked, I must have been slow on the uptake, usually I know when I am not wearing anything. I rushed back into the room, grabbed at a tea shirt and track suit bottoms, picked up some trainers and started to knock on all of the doors of my floor to make sure that everyone was awake and could find their way to the fire escape. Martin my manager was the only exception to this mass exodus, he and I cautiously opened the fire door and made our way down the flight of stairs to the floor below. We descended to the third floor and found that one of the guests had taken matters in hand and was organising the evacuation. Actually he was making a good job of it, some people were searching rooms, others were helping guests to exit via the fire escape, all calm and efficient.

Martin and I descended to the second floor, where nothing moved. Nobody had left their room, the only sound was the alarm ringing loud enough to wake the dead. I was really anxious to know what damage was being done to the hotel so left Martin on the second floor to organise things and went down into the lobby. I rushed to the bar, all was quiet, no fire there, I ran to the dining room, no fire there, I went into the kitchens, still no sign of any fire.

The hotel's alarm system is a fairly sophisticated one. There were sensors over the building linked with sprinklers and twenty-three alarm buttons which were placed behind little boxes with glass fronts. To set the alarm off, one broke the glass and pushed. The whole system was controlled by a master unit situated behind the reception desk. This master unit showed if any of the buttons had been pushed, or if any of the sensors detected fire. I glanced at the unit and halted in my tracks; the alarm button which had been pressed, which woke up the whole hotel, was the one in the lobby a few feet away from me, yet there was no sign of any fire that I could see. By this time several more people were trying to find the source of the blaze, they gathered in front of me comparing notes. Nobody has seen any trace of a fire or the smell of any smoke. I asked them to check again systematically, sending one off to the service yard at the rear of the property, one to the kitchens, another into the bars and yet another to the lounge. I went into the street to peer up at the facade of the hotel, all looked as it should. It might need another coat of paint within the next year but that was another problem. There was no fire, there was no smoke.

We reported back to one another that no fire could be found. What is more, the person who pressed the button triggering the system was not around as one might expect, it appears it had been a false alarm. D.C.I. Blake's words came floating back into my head "Every night the fire alarm would awaken everyone" perhaps it was a coincidence. Mr Jenkins could hardly attack the Bull from the grave.

I manually overrode the system, turned off the alarm, persuaded everyone to go back to bed saying a drunk had punched through the glass and had pushed the button. It was over an hour before the hotel regained its calm and peace descended once more; I did not regain my calm, what with Charles's behaviour, the murder and now the alarm; heavens what might happen next.

Could I sleep, I could not. I tried to read but still I lay awake tossing and turning: as soon as dawn broke, I dressed, jumped onto my bike and headed east; driving the eighty miles and casting off my cares as I went. Arriving at Colchester I passed one or two people who were still awake from the night before. I said good morning to them, they said goodnight to me. My room was a haven, I changed, went for a jog, fast, long, intensive, trying to get rid of some of the stress and emotion inside me. Then I flopped into bed and slept.

◈ CHAPTER 8 ◈

In fact I flopped onto rather than into my bed, and dozed off, not waking until almost noon. I stretched and stretched, went to the loo and then padded into the kitchen for a cup of coffee and piece of toast, still wearing my track suit. In the kitchen was Mel, who was also studying history although quite a different period, her interest lay in the twentieth century. Mel was leaning against the sink unit, dishevelled hair and drinking coffee; a ready listener. We had never actually been close friends but always stopped for a chat when we bumped into each other. Usually she was good company.

'Morning,' she said.

'How's you?' I asked.

'What a night, what a night. Oh my head.'

'As good as that eh, here have a glass of water.'

'A glass of water, why?'

'You are probably dehydrated, that in part, causes the hangover.'

'Really. How's things with you? You look a bit down.'

'Apart from a murder in my hotel, an idiot setting the burglar alarm off in the small hours of this morning, waking up the whole hotel unnecessarily and someone who I thought was my boyfriend having done the dirty on me, I suppose everything is fine, it just doesn't feel it.'

'Men are buggers, why don't you try a different softer more gentle and much more fun approach to life,' she said putting her arm around me and giving me a little squeeze.

I smiled at her and said that I wasn't of that persuasion, she told me it was a pity and to keep an open mind.

We chatted some more, I confess I poured my problems into her ear. She made the correct sort of noises, said that she agreed with me, that men were rotten, which isn't quite what I said. Mel made it quite clear that she thought my future really lay in cuddling ladies.

I returned to my room, alone incidentally, and showered. Dressed in a light green tee shirt and a short dark green skirt, I was going to wear jeans but decided against it, I made my way to the common room where there is always someone to chat to, and always the day's newspapers to scan through. Matthew was there and we were soon in easy conversation.

He said, 'hello you.'

'Matthew is it you then?' I asked the obvious. 'Is this seat taken?'

'If it was taken, it wouldn't be there.'

I smiled, sat and asked him how he was.

He complained of being lethargic, and feeling bored, unusual for him. I suggested a walk.

'I seldom walk,' he said. 'We could jog or we could drive.'

'The idea is to get some gentle exercise, not to reach a destination. In this instance, it is the journey that counts. A bit like life.'

'Where are you suggesting we walk, just around the campus?'

'Let's walk to Wivenhoe,' I suggested. Wivenhoe being a small village on the banks of the River Colne. When I first went there it was enchanting but recent development has not improved its attractiveness. Around the quay it is still quaint, and makes a pleasant amble.

'It's miles.'

'It's about two miles, that's all. Come on you, stir your great limbs.'

We set off gamely enough, chatting about sports and holidays, computers and hotels, gardening and handbags. It was light banter.

'I had an embarrassing experience yesterday,' he said. 'At lunch time I went to the Student's Union bar and bought myself a pint. It was a bit crowded, someone was making a fool of himself mucking about, he bumped into one of his friends and the friend bumped into me, a sort of domino effect. The consequence was that my beer landed in my lap, drenching my trousers. Everyone laughed, he apologised but his apology didn't dry me off. I had to slip away. I went to the university's launderette just around the corner which was deserted at that time of day, slipped off my jeans, and put them in the machine to rinse through. I was reading a newspaper just sitting in my underwear, as the Dean and some guests he was showing around the college, walked in. I did feel a fool.'

'Caught with your trousers down.'

'Caught in flagrante delicto.'

The walk was mainly down hill, soon we were walking through the upper village, then down to the bank of the river.

'Did you know I am a member of the University Sailing Club?' said Matthew.

'You are a man of many parts. Do you race?'

'Oh yes, mainly dinghys at present. They are fast, lots of fun, and very competitive. We race against each other either here or at Brightlingsea, the river is quite narrow in parts, too narrow to race cruisers and I couldn't afford one anyway. I should like to buy a flying fifteen dinghy sometime, but they are pricey. Usually about ten of us, sometimes more, have races either against each other using the club's lasers, or against a team from another club. We have a drink or two afterwards, it is convivial and fun.'

'It must be difficult to start to learn to sail with all those ropes and knots?'

'Not at all. If you go out with an experienced sailor who can explain everything slowly, and if the weather is not to blustery, it is easy to pick up the basics after an hour or two. Our club has a small sailing yacht at present moored off Wivenhoe, I think it's much easier to learn on a cruiser, things happen much more slowly.'

The quay itself was teeming with people, it being Sunday afternoon. We strolled along exploring, chatting looking at the fleet racing half a mile or so away, Matthew nodding to a few of his acquaintances. There were three white poles set up and he explained to me the starting procedure using these as marker posts. We walked on until we came across a tiny rowing boat with the words 'Tender to Snowflake' written in white paint across it's tiny stern.

'Snowflake is the name of our cruiser, the club cruiser,' said Matthew. 'It seems nobody is using her today, let's take a look.'

'How do you know nobody is using her?'

'We always use this tender to get out to her, as she lies in deep water, if the tender is here, there is nobody on board.'

He pushed the boat down to the waters edge, jumped in, then put an oar in each of the rowlocks. He held the boat steady for me to climb in. I wish I had kept my jeans on. With surprising ability he rowed us out into the stream, then along for a few hundred yards until he allowed the boat to drift onto a dirty white craft with a tiny cabin, a mast and a boom. The boom had a sail tied tightly around it.

'Snowflake always looks dirty from the outside, mainly because of the seagulls, they're a nuisance but they are part of the scene down here. The inside of the boat is kept in a much better condition, we are particular about it but even that smells a bit musty to begin with.'

Matthew tied the two boats together, using he said, a bowline, left his shoes and socks in the tender, and climbed aboard leaving me sitting contentedly in the boat, gently bobbing up and down but my tranquillity wasn't to last.

'Come and see over her,' he said.

'I am quite happy here.'

'No, no, come and have a peep.'

I stood up really carefully taking care not to push my feet, which were in the tender, away from my hands which were on the cruiser, I am not much of a mariner but I knew that much. Somehow I wriggled aboard, and sat on the deck at the rear of the boat. There was a winch or two, some cord, and to my left, what must be the entrance to the cabin but it was well and truly locked. The sail swung gently above my head.

I looked back at the land, some 50 meters way, or perhaps it wasn't that far. There were boats of all sizes nearly all sailing boats, criss crossing the stretch of water in front of me, just missing each other by a hairs breadth. All very pretty. Suddenly I felt at peace with the world, actually being on the water was delightful, I realised the attraction of messing about with boats. I thought we might just stay afloat for a few moments then make our return journey but Matthew was anxious to show me all over Snowflake. He had disappeared somewhere up towards the bow, and came back clutching a key.

'We always keep a spare key tied to the mooring line,' he said, 'Here we are.'

He found the padlock's key hole, gave a twist, and pushed back the hatch cover. Once the hatch cover was released three interlocking wooden sections which acted as a door to the cabin, could be lifted out one by one revealing a short set of steps. Matthew descended to the cabin, drew back the curtains, and smiled.

Chapter 8

'There you are, welcome aboard Snowflake, isn't she sweet. She is just a training vessel but we have outings on her, picnics and so on and use her as a committee boat. I put my head around the doorway and saw a neat cabin with a few charts rolled up and protruding in one locker. There was no cooker or washing facilities on view but a number of sail bags were stuffed at the bow end. A well polished pole extended from ceiling to floor, Matthew said it carried the weight of the mast to the keel and no doubt that was correct.

He held my hand and led me into the cabin, I sat on the bunk with his arm loosely around my waist.

'What do you think of her?' he said, a bit like a proud father.

'I expected her to smell a bit more than she does. She is quite cosy, nice soft bunks, I thought you would have a cooker.'

'Cookers are difficult, they need to be kept clean, if you have a cooker, you need pots and pans, somewhere to keep food, knives and forks and a gas supply. Much better, when numerous people share a boat, to have just cold food and a thermos and bring it with you each time.'

He came closer and kissed my cheek, decision time for me I thought.

'What are you after Matthew?'

'A cuddle,' he said.

'Cuddles can have strings attached to them,' I heard myself saying.

137

'No strings,' he promised, easing me along so that I was laying on the bunk rather than sitting on it, but still I had my feet on the floor.

He put his hand on my knee and brought his fingers up my leg touching me to within an inch or two of my thong.

'I heard a story once,' I said putting my hand on top of his to prevent things going too quickly, 'Of a lady smacking a gentleman's hand when he did that, she said, "Excuse me, breasts first for heavens sake".'

'Oh!' said Matthew.

'Just teasing,' I said.

'But it's a good idea.'

'He kissed my lips, and I kissed him back, he put his arms around me, then nibbled at my ear. One hand caressed my breast, covered as it was in only a tee shirt and my bra. He slipped his hand under my tee shirt and fondled me gently, then slipped it down my bra his fingers finding my nipple. I wriggled a little so that my tee shirt wrinkled up, he cupped his hand under my breast and drew it free from my clothes, then he took my nipple in his mouth and played with me, meanwhile his hand roamed down the side of my body. As all this took place on part of a narrow bunk and I was doubled up, my feet still on the floor, not much was going to happen without considerable co-operation. I sat up and looked at him, I was fond of him, not in love with him, but fond of him.

'What's the matter?' he asked 'I haven't offended you have I? You know I want you.'

'We need some ground rules,' I said sitting up.

'Ground rules?'

'I am not in the mood for a quick grope. I would like some loving, gentle, soft, romantic.'

'Won't argue with that.'

I stroked his hair, and fondled an ear. I made him lie down and I snuggled up to him, one of his hands went down my back and held my bottom but more a gesture to stop me falling off the bunk on to the cabin floor, than a sexual move; or was it? We kissed again, quite tenderly.

'I have always loved you,' he said stroking me. I looked into his eyes.

'It's good to be loved,' I said. We were really close, intertwined our arms, legs, even our breath. There was not a millimetre between our clothes, but it wasn't really very comfortable, as I was lying on an arm which had nowhere to go. Slowly I sat up, I made him lie down, and eased myself on top of him. We kissed again he stroked me but it was still very unsatisfactory. The bunk itself was small, to accommodate a sleeping adult; a hole had been cut away in the bulkhead for leg room but there was insufficient room for four legs. We both sat up looking dishevelled.

I was getting more and more turned on. We are going to have problems unless I change position, and make life a little easier. My good intentions drifted away.

'I have an idea, would you replace two of the door panels over there, but leave the third, and the hatch cover open.'

Obviously a bit mystified he got up and inserted two of the three panels into their slots. Whilst he was doing that, I slipped my arms out of my tee shirt unclipped by bra and took it off, and put my arms back in. I stood up, with my elbows resting on the top of the panels, so that I was facing out of the cabin. I was now wearing a short skirt, a thong, my tee shirt, and a smile.

'I am all yours,' I said, 'but be gentle, and nothing kinky.'

'Ah.'

He nuzzled up to me, his face against my back, his hands touching the outside of my legs. He raised his hands, put a finger either side of my thong, and pulled it down and off. All I wore now was a very short skirt and a tee shirt. He raised my skirt I felt his fingers press against my skin just at the base of my spine, then travel slowly down my bum, between my legs and into me. To help him I bent forwards just a little. Then he covered me with kisses, at least, that part of me usually concealed beneath my skirt, he oh so gently massaged the lips of my vagina with two of his fingers and then stopped to unzip himself. I was still gazing out to sea, but felt him against me, and then enter me, he was much bigger than I imagined he would be. As we made love his hands felt under my tee shirt and held a breast in each.

I thought he would come to a climax too quickly for me so I stopped him after a few moments, turned round, and put my arms around him.

'Nice and slowly,' I said.

Chapter 8

'I sat him down on the bunk and looked at him. Men always seem ungainly when they are half undressed, mind you, many men aren't too gainly wholly undressed, fortunately Matthew was an exception, he had a fine body and was quite large where it really mattered. He took his clothes off and then looked to me to know what I wanted him to do next. I sat him down on the bunk, then sat down on his knee with my back towards him.

'It's called the chaperone position,' I said as he was settling into me, 'in the days of yester year very few people wore knickers. A game lady would hike up her skirts, before sitting on a gentleman's lap. The gentleman would then be in a position to accommodate her without the chaperone knowing what was afoot.'

'What was afoot eh,' he said.

'Either that or what was ... oh that's very nice.'

'What me inside you or me scratching your back?'

'You scratching my back of course.'

'I think I hate you.'

'Then I'll wriggle a bit more.'

Just at that moment a largish motor boat came past, its wake causing the Snowflake to wallow, which caused us to wallow, which caused us both to come to a climax.

Respectability returned to us as we made our way to the shore, we walked back to the campus hand in hand.

'Let's have supper together,' he said. 'I'll take you out somewhere.'

'O.K.' I said 'but we will each pay for ourselves.'

'But I ..,' he started.

'We each pay for ourselves,' I said firmly.

Matthew and I parted company at the quadrangle, I made my way to my rooms. We had agreed to meet up again at 7 o'clock for a drink then we might go on to eat somewhere. I walked through the university campus nodding to one or two people I knew. I walked on towards the block where my room was situated, in front of the block were some stone steps, and on one of these steps sat Charles. He got up as soon as he saw me, he wasn't in a smiling mood, but by then nor was I.

'What are you doing here?' I asked.

'Did you read my letter?'

'I don't want anything to do with you.'

'Too right, but I insist on putting the record straight. You overheard part of my conversation and you think I was asking Sharon out for a date, and because of that you got mad at me.'

'I did hear you ask her out.'

'You may have heard me suggesting she came round to my house and why on earth shouldn't she, she is my cousin.'

'Your cousin!'

'When my family came down to live in Hackney, we stayed with my mother's sister for about six months, she is my aunt, Sharon her daughter, is my cousin. After those six months we were given a council house in the next street and we were always in and out of each other's houses. Then my aunt was moved by the council to Stevenage New Town and we lost contact a bit. When I qualified, my aunt told me that she had made enquiries and there didn't seem to be an equine dentist around that part of North Hertfordshire, so again I stayed at their house this time in Stevenage whilst I set up shop. Eventually I moved into digs, as I didn't want to outstay my welcome, they only had a three bedroomed semi. Later I shared with a friend, I have my own house now as I told you but I had not seen Sharon for a while and invited her round for a chat. They are a super family, they have always been kind to me and I have never had the chance to repay them. I have tried to see you to tell you this after you threw the wine at me but you wouldn't let me in, I have tried to explain all this on the telephone but you put the receiver down, I have written but you did not read my letter. I am really cheesed off with you.'

Charles said all this really quickly, he was obviously very upset indeed, and when he finished he just marched off, leaving me dumbfounded, feeling a heel, and feeling dreadful. Oh dear. I started to walk after him but his pace was twice that of mine, he reached his van, and just drove off without a backwards glance. Ouch.

Mournfully I walked back to my rooms, lay on my bed and wondered what on earth I had done. I really regretted my afternoon with Matthew, I really regretted jumping at conclusions with Charles, hell. And Charles was such a nice person, I had obviously hurt him deeply. I cried a bit and felt very lonely.

I thought that perhaps the way forward was to write to Charles, and started a letter, but couldn't think what to say apart from the fact that I was sorry. Looking around the room I caught sight his letter to me, with trepidation I opened it and read that he thought I ought to give him time to explain, that I should not have jumped to conclusions. He told me in his letter that he had lived with his aunt and that Sharon was his cousin, that she had a boyfriend of long standing, and that his suggestion of meeting her at his house was platonic, the invitation extended to her boyfriend if he was free. It was just a family event, of no emotional consequences, or should have been if I had not eavesdropped. The letter I eventually wrote, after many false starts, would, I hope, patch things up between us. I slipped out to telephone Caroline for Charles's address, completed the envelope and put a stamp in the corner.

I felt worse, and I was due to meet Matthew again that evening.

Mechanically I washed, dressed into jeans and a jumper and walked out of the room to meet Matthew in the common room. Half way to the common room I realised I had left the room without money, and even worse, especially in my present state, without make up. I was going to pieces. Hurrying back, I daubed something thick and powdery on my face, something pink on my lips, stuffed a hanky and a twenty pound note in my pocket, ran a comb through my hair and set off again.

I met Matthew as I had promised to do, at 7 o'clock just outside the sports hall, although my heart was not in the rendezvous. I decided to wear black jeans with black tee shirt under a black jumper I bought in Hitchin; coincidentally the day of the murder. The jumper was an impulse buy, I had not worn it previously, but black suited my mood that evening. We were both punctual, and totally ignored our intimacy of the afternoon. Matthew drove us to a small pub near Brightlingsea down tiny country roads with which he seemed very familiar. I must admit it was delightful, both the countryside and our watering hole which was full of people who had spent the day sailing. They were very enthusiastic and their enthusiasm did rub off. Everyone around me seemed to know one another, and were chatting about buoys and tides and gybing, and why one boat was a little faster than another. Who was doing what.

The pub was an old one, heaven knows how old, with all the things that old pubs should have including beams and brasses. I sat down at one of the few empty tables whilst Matthew ordered our drinks, a beer for him, a glass of white wine for me, and our food, there seemed to be quite a crush at the bar. We were having steak and chips, mine a bit under done, his a bit over done, at least to my taste. When ordering and paying for the food, the barmaid had given Matthew a huge wooden spoon with a number on it. He said he was told to listen for a waitress calling out the number, and she would bring the food over; nothing unusual in that. Our number was 24, and sure enough, after about 35 minutes a waitress holding a large tray called out number 24 but the food on the tray was not ours. The waitress said it had to be our food as we held the wooded spoon with number 24 on it. We pointed out that on the tray were three meals and there were only two of us; that we had ordered steaks, but the food on the tray was a mixture of scampi, gammon steak and what was probably vegetable bake.

Hearing our conversation, the rightful owners of the food, waving a wooden spoon with 23 on it, came up and directed the waitress their way. Reluctantly she complied. Very shortly afterwards, another waitress called out number 23 and she held a tray containing two steaks and chips. The steak was on very hot trivets, they were still sizzling.

We cleared enough room on the table, and set too; ignoring the waitress who said it wasn't our food but food belonging to number 23.

Such a mix up over wooden spoons of all things may not sound over exciting, probably common place indeed it sounds prosaic even to me but it set me thinking.

'You are not with me, are you?' said Matthew after a moment or two. I realised he had been talking to me.

'Sorry,' I said, 'let me explain. I told you about the murder at my hotel, I told you that the murdered man, Richard Jenkins was in Room 26. What I did not tell you, and until now I had not appreciated the significance of the fact, was that earlier that day there had been a mix up over the keys. Ian my work experience lad, who was on reception at the time, had given keys to Room 16 to Mr Barrett, and keys to Room 26 to Mr Jenkins, whereas on the computer Mr Barrett was registered as being in Room 26 and Mr Jenkins was registered in Room 16. I did not realise until much later that Ian had not corrected the computer properly.

What happened is that the two guests arrived at the same time and both checked in at the same time. Ian says he put both sets of keys on top of the reception desk and each guest picked up a set of keys. As it happened each picked up the keys which were earmarked for the other. That meant if someone checked on the computer to see in which room Mr Barrett was in, they would have been given Mr Jenkin's room number, just supposing the wrong man was murdered.'

'That's hardly likely to have happened is it? It is not often that the wrong man is murdered.'

'About as likely as getting the wrong wooden spoon in this pub I should think,' I said.

'Ah! Yes I see. I suppose it's possible. Does that help you find out who the murderer is.'

'Unhappily I think it makes it more difficult. The murderer would have had to have access to our main computer, which means either an inside job, God forbid, or someone telephoning reception to check who was in which room, and being told the wrong room. I think I should telephone D.C.I. Blake immediately. I expect he already knows, but it may be important.'

'At least wait until you have finished eating.'

'That sounds wise, it does taste good. Tell me more about sailing.'

'Sailing, yes. It is addictive. If you don't have too many days without wind, or too many days with too much wind, or too many days when the tide is wrong, it is good, provided your crew doesn't let you down. The other members of the club are interesting folk, we have got to know each other fairly well over the months. Would you like to come along sometime?'

'Do you know, I rather think I might, but strictly to learn about ropes and sails.'

We chatted on, I brightened up a little.

❧ CHAPTER 9 ❧

Monday morning again, I could not believe another week had passed, they always say that time passes more quickly for the elderly, I felt rather old and world weary. Same old routine, up betimes, whenever that is, but it is mentioned in Samuel Pepys diaries and off for a jog which wasn't very satisfactory as it was so blustery. It's difficult to run in windy weather. Then showered, breakfasted and dressed in black jeans with my brown leather jacket over a white shirt I read history for an hour or so before I ventured out again. Most of my history reading passed with fascination yet occasionally I hit a dull spot and this was one of them. I was reading about the concept behind the structure of the government at that time and the best way for me to remember everything was to make copious notes as I went along, then to revise those notes three or four hours later, then the next day, then a week later. This, coupled with flash cards with which I tested myself periodically, allowed facts to sink into my brain. I so envied people who could memorise with ease.

At 11 o'clock I walked to my lecture for a talk on twelfth and thirteenth century land holdings presumably in case we wanted to be twelfth and thirteenth century lawyers. Actually it was quite interesting, all about the Statute of Westminster, it seems there were three of them cleverly numbered First, enacted in 1275, Second enacted 1285 and Third enacted 1290. The effect of these statutes trickled down the ages so it was very relevant indeed to my reading. More notes to take back to my room and rewrite, more flash cards to prepare and use.

The lecture ended, and everyone left the lecture hall as quickly as they could, it was as if they all had a train to catch. The lecturer stayed on for a bit talking to two people, everyone else exited left. Mel was there, and we found ourselves walking next to each other.

'Not much relevance to the twentieth century Mel,' I said.

'Maybe, maybe not, but he's a first class lecturer, and can make the dullest subject sound interesting. Don't forget that much of our land law didn't change until the end of the nineteenth century and the beginning of the twentieth century. The sweeping legislation was the Law of Property Acts 1922 and 1925, these old laws were very relevant indeed at the beginning of the twentieth century.'

'Have you anything planned today apart from work?'

'I'm going into Colchester later on, perhaps after lunch. You're most welcome to come. I have some friends there and we're having lunch together.'

'Not another of your girlie days Mel?' said Judy who was walking just behind.

'Could be, what are you doing today Judy?' said Mel.

'I hope I'm going shopping in Ipswich. My father's driving down, and promised to take me out.'

'You can't take your father shopping, he'll want to see round Colchester Castle, or visit the coast.'

Chapter 9

We nattered on for a while my classmates and me before making our way to Cafe Vert for a coffee. At least that was our intention, but I failed to make it that day.

Halfway across the square I was approached by a middle aged man dressed in a dark suit, unusual on the campus. The man called me by name but I didn't recognise him at first, although as soon as he introduced himself I realised that I should have known him but it's not always easy to recognise relative strangers if they are in a setting different to the one you are used to seeing them in. It was Mr Barrett.

'Good morning Miss White,' he said.

'Excuse me, do I know you?' I said.

'It's me, Jeffrey Barrett, we've met several times, at your hotel, at the Bull.'

'Good heavens, Mr Barrett, what are you doing here?'

'I've driven over to see you. Might we have a word please, in private?' he said.

'You want a word with me in private?'

'Yes, that would be wonderful.'

I looked about me, where could we go. I didn't like the idea of inviting him back to my rooms although I was sure he was harmless enough. One of the coffee shops might do but it was hardly private, where else was there? The common room would be full.

'Let's go back into the lecture theatre, it's at least empty now, if rather huge for just the two of us to talk,' I said, leading him back to the room I had just left. We both sat down, in adjoining seats half turned to each other, the seating was raked for lectures and not ideal for a confidential discussion, but it did.

'A word in private, you said.'

'This is very serious, I want to explain something to you, something both important, and secret, but before doing so, I want you to telephone D.C.I. Blake in Hitchin. Is there a telephone here somewhere?'

'Yes I suppose so,' I said, 'but why should I want to telephone the police?'

'Please, humour me, it is very important indeed and he will explain to you. As I say, I've driven from Hitchin just to speak to you but before I go into things, I do ask please that you make that telephone call,' said Jeffrey Barrett.

I looked at him, he seemed very troubled, and looked much older than when I had last spoken to him.

'Am I in any danger?' I asked.

'No, it is not that, but please make the call.'

There was no telephone in the lecture room, the nearest one that I could use was in the adjacent offices. I walked over to it and dialled the number Jeffrey Barrett had given me, I was put through first to Pretty Assistant, and then to D.C.I. Blake himself. It was almost as if he had been waiting for the call.

'Ah Miss White,' he said, 'Thank you for calling, this is all rather important. First of all I want to make sure you recognise my voice.'

'Yes inspector, I recognise your voice.'

Chapter 9

'Mr Barrett wants to discuss things with you. I want you to promise that the only person you will repeat what he says to you, is me or my assistant. That is very important.'

'Very well Inspector,' I said.

'Secondly, I want to tell you that he is employed by the security service and you can discuss the case with him, in the same manner that you might discuss it with me, he has been made fully aware of what has happened at your hotel.'

'Yes but why?'

'He will explain it all to you,' said the Inspector.

'Very well.'

And the 'phone went dead. Slowly I made my way back to the lecture theatre, half expecting Mr Barrett to have disappeared but he was still there sitting in exactly the same position as when I had left him.

'This is all a little mysterious Mr Barrett,' I said as I approached him.

'It is all very serious too,' he said. 'This had to be confidential, normally we would not be having this conversation at all but your actions over the last 24 hours have altered things greatly.'

'My actions!' I was alarmed, was my love making in Snowflake known to everyone?

'Let me start at the beginning. This is highly confidential. I work for the security services, trying to get evidence to prosecute drug traffickers. It is quite dangerous, it is not very pleasant but if we can secure a conviction it will be wonderful.

I have been working on the case for over two years, pretending to be a trafficker myself. If they ever find out who I am, they will probably kill me.

As far as I know my cover has not been blown, but then you come up with the suggestion that the person intended to be murdered at the Bull, was me, not Jenkins.'

'I was only trying to be helpful.'

'We are not complaining but several threads have now come unentwined. Many people would try to murder me if they knew of my real identity,' said Mr Barrett.

'There we are then, it was probably one of those,' I said.

'Maybe, or maybe not, the people who I might fear are really unlikely to poison me, that's not how they operate at all. They might use guns, possibly knives, possibly an iron bar, but not poison. It's almost inconceivable that anyone wishing to kill me would try to poison me, and yet it seems possible that it has happened. If it has happened, it means that my cover may have been blown, which makes my life expectancy quite short; but then, nobody has tried to kill me again. You can now appreciate my difficulties and the danger I might be in.'

'I hate to seem ungracious but that is your problem.'

'Of course it is and I am not asking you to share it with me. First of all, I am really anxious that you do not speak about this to anyone. Please do not share your thoughts with another sole except for D.C.I. Blake or myself. Secondly, I need you to run through the murder scenario again, to tell me how the keys were changed. Thirdly, I need to question you about the hotel procedure.'

'But I have told D.C.I. Blake all this, at least twice now, surely I don't have to repeat it all over again,' I said.

'Yes, but then it was from the angle that Jenkins was the victim. The focus of attention has now moved and it's much more deadly from my point of view.'

It took quite a while, going through the whole story again. What Mr Barrett made of it, I do not know, he said very little, but certainly looked perplexed. He made jottings whilst I was talking, and when I had finished he asked me for the list of females who had been employed by the hotel, in any capacity, during the last six years. This was obtainable from the hotel's computer records, it took a little while and I had to insist Gloria gave it priority. After not too long a wait we were given a list of 43 ladies, two of whom unfortunately had died and three of whom had emigrated. I had not realised how important lists were in crime solving. Quite how one might sift through the remaining 38 souls remaining on this new list was not clear, if it was a sham chambermaid who had delivered the wine, if she had been employed in the hotel, then presumably it could be any one of them. That, thank goodness, was not my problem.

'How can you be so sure it's not me?' I asked.

'Frankly we are not at all sure, in the sense that we are keeping an open mind.'

'Then why trust me with your secret.'

'If it was you, then you know the secret already. If it wasn't you, then provided you honour your pledge to remain silent, the secret will remain a secret. We do know that you are not a gossip.'

'Is that a compliment?'

'If you like.'

We chatted on and then he left, still looking a worried man.

Meeting Jeffrey Barrett and hearing what he had to say left me restless. I didn't want exercise, I wasn't tired, it was too early for a drink. I was not in the mood to transcribe the rough lecture notes into my own words to start the process of getting the points to stick in my brain, getting them into my long-term memory from my short-term memory. I needed to be distracted. I wandered back to my rooms with no real purpose in mind, it was now too late to join my friends in the cafe. I opened my door to find a message from Matthew lying on the mat.

'Saun and I are taking Snowflake out for a jaunt this afternoon, why not join us. We will teach you to sail, bring a change of clothes.' The message read. So I did.

We met up in the car park, clambered into Matthew's Volkswagen and set off this time for Brightlingsea where it seems Snowflake is usually berthed.

We reached the quayside in considerably different weather conditions to that of my last visit to Snowflake. It was windy, not just a breeze but stormy, a real blow much too strong for sailing to my mind but what did I know.

'It seems very windy.' I said hoping that they might take the hint.

'Yes. Force 6 I should think. It has freshened quite considerably since this morning.'

'How do you know it's force 6, you're just saying that.'

'Not at all. The beaufort wind scale is quite specific. Each wind force has different pointers. Force 6 is when you have large waves developing with foamy crests and spray. Large tree branches move and you can hear the wind whistling in the telephone wires. That is what we can see and hear this afternoon.'

'That's wonderful.'

'Yes, I also telephoned the weather station before we left campus just to check.'

'Isn't it too windy to go out.'

'Heavens no, it should be exciting. We can always put a reef in the sail if we are overpowered.'

'How often do you do that.'

'Never so far but today might be the first time. Things are going to happen fast today, I am not sure how much you are going to learn.'

There wasn't much to carry from the parked car to the tender, three sports bags, and two coolie bins, the sea looked very uninviting, I couldn't think how we were even going to launch the tender, let alone sail Snowflake. Indeed it took the efforts of both Saun and Matthew to pull the tender into the water, then to push her off and jump in. I was very much the passenger and expected to remain so throughout the day. With each of them taking an oar, we came alongside Snowflake and very ungainly I was pushed aboard. I scrambled over the decking with someone's hand pushing me from behind. Spray was covering the deck, and me.

'You have a very squashy rear,' shouted Saun over the whining of the wind in the rigging, and the slapping of the water against the hull.

'You shouldn't be feeling it,' I said, 'And if you do have to push me aboard like that, you needn't mention it,' but I don't think he either heard or cared. He was busy passing stuff from the tender to Matthew who was now standing on Snowflake's deck, both boats pulled at their moorings. I was directed into the cabin and everything was passed down to me, at least there I was out of the wind and spray. I was handed the chilly bins and the sports bags and I was told to stow everything on the cabin floor where it would be safe. Matthew set about checking the bilges, we all donned life jackets. It was going to be rough, the bottom third section of the door was left in place to stop excess water swamping the cabin.

Fast, furious activity then took place all around me, I sat on the deck out of the way and watched. It was noisy, very noisy with the boats slapping against each other, the rigging resounding to the wind, ropes and cleats slapping against the mast and the sea crashing around us. Saun started unleashing the main sail, which flapped and shook trying to escape from his clutches. Matthew was busy sorting out the foresail and within a short space of time we had actually cast off and were turning to face towards the land.

'I thought we were going down towards the open sea,' I said.

'We need to get the boats head into the wind, so we can raise and secure the sails properly.' explained Saun. This we did or at least, they did whilst I kept out of the way but failed to dodge the spray which came right over the top of the cabin.

Suddenly we swept round again and we were sailing down stream, I realised what attracted so many people to sailing boats. The boat was carried along on the crest of one wave, then that wave dropped us and we seemed to be waiting for the next. It was much gentler than I expected it to be considering the strength of the wind.

'We are on a broad reach,' said Matthew, 'Things will be very different when we eventually turn into the wind.'

'Lunch time,' said Saun.

'I thought we were going to stop, I pictured us moored up in some delightful cove only accessible by boat,' I said.

'It's much too rough for that today. Would you butter some bread? Two slices each will do for a start, we once took one lady for a sail, she was so frightened when the boat heeled that she buttered the whole loaf, on both sides of the bread, without even realising what she was doing. It was a very messy picnic that day. Butter got everywhere.' We all laughed.

'You'll find some sliced ham, some sliced cheese, tomatoes and apples. There is also some fudge, fingers of cake and coffee and a pot of strawberry jam. Water as well if you're thirsty.'

'Saun buys exactly the same picnic every time we go out. He usually adds that the jam is from local strawberries.'

'Why do you always buy the same food?' I asked Saun.

'It saves any mental effort, it is suitable for vegetarians if they're aboard, everyone can find something they can eat, it's not too expensive and it's not frilly.'

'I've never had a frilly picnic.'

'You must have, there are always napkins, proper glasses not the polystyrene ones we use, the crusts are cut off the cucumber sandwiches, the whole thing is dainty.'

'Hang on, we must go about,' said Matthew.

'Aren't you going to gybe?' said Saun.

'Not today.'

Matthew pushed the tiller over, pulling in sails at the same time, we went all the way round, eventually and only after a great deal of noise from the sails, we faced about ninety degrees from our last course. It was all done very competently.

I set about making sandwiches, on a heaving boat with all of the ingredients set about the cabin floor. I took a paper plate, and lay a piece of bread on it but it quickly slipped off. I had to hold the bread on the plate with one hand and then take the lip of the butter substitute with the other, holding the tub between my knees. I needed a third hand to butter the bread and to undo the packet of ham. Somehow I coped and cut the sandwich into quarters. Offering up my efforts, which quickly became wet with sea water, I enquired why they didn't simplify matters and buy ready made sandwiches.

'But you would then be unemployed,' said Saun.

'I think I could put up with that.'

Sitting, happily between the two of them, munching our food I asked Saun.

'What do you do?'

'I'm a drug councillor. At one level I try to get people to stop taking drugs, at another I sit on various committees to advise on how best to tackle the drug problem. My background is psychology I took my degree at Queen's in Belfast.'

'What are you doing in Colchester?'

'My PhD. It's a three-year course. I'm working on drugs, in particular crack. Why people take them, how best to try to get them to give them up. That sort of thing.'

'Is it interesting?'

'I think the human mind is always interesting, academically it is fascinating but most of the people I see are very sad, usually poor in both spirit and money; they do not even realise how far into the mire they have sunk. Those on crack, crack cocaine, are often the worse, it's a dreadful substance which the human mind really can't cope with.'

'I have never really understood it.'

'In essence cocaine comes from the coca plant that grows in

South America. The Indians use to put coca leaves into their mouths and chewed them swallowing the juices, not too much harm with that but scientists learnt how to extract pure cocaine and that's crazy stuff. I think it's much worse than heroin and that is bad enough. Cannabis is quite mild in comparison.'

At that moment a gust appeared from a different quarter making Snowflake yawl at an alarming pitch, both Matthew and Saun jumped to adjust sails and tiller. Water streamed over the thwart onto the deck where we were sitting but it didn't stay there long, it was drained off somewhere. I was going to ask about it but the moment passed whilst my companions were so busy, they didn't seem in any way troubled by the strength of the wind, the state of the sea or the seaworthiness of Snowflake. Neither of them noticed what they were eating, their minds were wholly on the wind, the tide and the boat.

'Would you like anything else to eat?' I asked.

'I'm cool,' said Saun.

'Me too,' echoed Matthew.

We sailed on, and shortly without me even realising it, we had made our way back to the mooring buoy and our jaunt was over. I had learnt virtually nothing in the way of how to handle a boat but we had enjoyed ourselves, I felt exhilarated and was very wet.

Whilst making our way back to shore in the tender I once again approached the subject of drugs but it was from a different angle.

'Saun, there can't be much trust in the drug world.'

'That's true. Lots of fear but little trust.'

'I have a picture of a poor farmer somewhere perhaps in Burma growing opium poppies. He takes the opium collected and sells it to a trader in Burma.'

'More or less, yes.' A wave a bit larger than the others swamped us, I was told to bail and found an old tin mug tied by a piece of twine to a hole in one of the ribs.

'This trader must then distribute it say to England.'

'It is often turned into heroin before shipment. Naive or desperate people called mules are used to take the drugs across the world, it doesn't matter to the trader if they get caught or not, they are expendable. The mules drop the drugs in what is hoped is a safe place, later they are picked up by a paid help. The paid helper gives the drugs to the English distributor usually the head of a gang.'

'Why does the trader trust the English distributor?'

'I imagine that the trade between them starts off in a very small way and slowly grows, often they are part of the same family. Why do you ask? This isn't really the aspect of drugs I study.'

'It's a bit confidential but if someone was trying to catch drug dealers, could they infiltrate the gang?'

'It's not easy but yes, over a period of time. Most of the gang members have known each other for many years, if they found someone else muscling in on their patch or if they found they were being betrayed, they would be ruthless.'

Instead of going straight back, we called in at the local tavern, and I was immediately accepted as one of the sailing fraternity. Perhaps my lack of make up, hair blown everywhere, ruddy complexion and being accompanied by Matthew and Saun had a lot to do with it. I was even asked how the seas had been that afternoon and the single word 'awesome' sealed my status. It seems nobody else had ventured out that day.'

❧ CHAPTER 10 ❧

Time passes. I took my masters degree successfully, leaving behind study and the relatively carefree life at Colchester University and headed for London as countless thousands of people have done before me. Little time or thought could be spared to probe further the problems of the murder of Richard Jenkins, I did not hear from D.C.I. Plod, nor Mr Barrett, the events during those hot summer days seemed to be a closed chapter in my life and would probably have remained so if it had not been for a strange set of circumstances. In London I rented a flat in Islington, and joined the commercial world by getting employment with a company called Shorts Ltd, a firm specialising in organising conferences, both large and small.

They were a good firm to work for, they knew exactly what they wanted and insisted on getting it for their clients. Their requirements, especially what they required from their staff, were exacting, they did not book second rate. Whilst organising one of their conferences nothing else must matter to the Short's representative of whom I was one. You could be ill, or take a holiday but only after the conference had finished: it wasn't that easy of course, for as soon as one conference had finished, another was on the way. They worked us hard.

I and all of my colleagues were each given a specific conference to oversee and oversee meant comprehensive organising from the venue and travel, to tying up speakers, menus and outings. Everything had to go like clockwork, excuses were not listened to, it became a habit to check and double check.

Shorts were very very good and very very expensive; they paid their staff, well, but expected total dedication and organising, a conference was not quite as easy as it may sound.

Save for the really large conferences, where a team of experts were sometimes employed, each conference was allocated to a particular member of staff on the taxi rank principle, it worked in this way. A list of members of staff would be made up and names entered at the bottom of this list as soon as the conference on which one was engaged, ended. The person whose name was at the top of the list at any particular time, was assigned the next conference to organise; whether it be London, Paris, St Petersburg or Margate. It might be a conference for five people or 300 people, it all depended on the luck of the draw, naturally the larger the conference, the more difficult it was to tie all of the loose ends together.

I had just finished organising a conference in Sorrento in Southern Italy. It had been a real pleasure. The delegates and the client were all delighted with the event, the weather had been gorgeous, the hotel efficient. There had been about one hundred delegates, none of whom had been taken ill, mugged or had been found, where they really didn't want to bc found, a euphemism for being caught with a young lady in one's room. These were the three usual problems met when a large number of gentlemen approaching middle age, spent a few days away at a conference. That conference had lasted for five days and the delegates had been kept occupied from breakfast time to early evening so I had free time to shop, swim, walk and explore.

Sometimes I would catch a bus to a small village and walk back as that way it was the bus that climbed the hill. Bus tickets initially proved a problem, they were not sold on the bus itself, nor at any obvious vending machine. In the end I had to ask at the hotel and was told the name of the shops where tickets were sold but they had to be bought before starting the journey. Confidentially the manager told me that nobody ever checked that tickets had been bought and really I needn't bother about buying one. Needless to say I did bother, that's my nature; indeed I bought a book of tickets at the first opportunity and just as well for an inspector was on the first bus I rode.

My lazy days were also spent jogging on a machine in the gym then lingering over breakfast before planning my outing for the day. In the evening I socialised with the delegates, no great hardship as many of them were very interesting and were quite amusing as well. Numerous invitations were pressed on me to spend an hour or a night with this or that delegate in his room, each invitation gently but firmly declined. My love life had been non-existent since my dalliance with Matthew on board Snowflake but I had no intention of fraternising with any of the delegates to that extent. The socialising called for an array of dresses, all paid for by Shorts. I never wore the same outfit twice when attending conferences. Short wanted the best and never begrudged paying expense accounts but each item had to be accompanied by an receipt, and that's how it should be. In Sorrento there were 100 delegates, each paid £725 a total of £72,500. That is a considerable sum of money earned by Shorts, increased incidentally, by payment being made to an offshore company by which, through an elaborate financial scheme to which I was not a party, the income escaped British Corporation Tax. I personally paid income tax in the usual way but it seems my services were hired out to a company resident in England which had many of the overall expenses assigned to its balance sheet but the only income it received was for conferences which actually took place in England.

In any event, I had to look very smart indeed, Shorts were quite happy to fork out for an expensive dress or two. If I were reported to have looked slovenly wearing perhaps jeans and a tee shirt or swim topless, it would soon be back to the big bosses and severely commented upon before I was out of the pool.

The five days of the Italian conference, the Italian Job as I called it, passed very quickly. As always I was the last to leave the hotel as it was part of my responsibility to make sure that nobody had left anything behind, all bar bills properly settled, nothing stolen. Shorts were as anxious to retain its excellent reputation with the hotel proprietors as much as with the delegates and the client companies. They wanted their good name to spread. The flight back to England, in first class of course, was a delight, I was quite looking forward to my next assignment.

In accordance with historic procedure at Shorts, my name was placed at the bottom of the list of operatives who had completed their current tasks, and would work its way to the top. This was called the wall-paper chart as originally clerks had kept the records on a roll of wall-paper slowly rolling up one end and unrolling the other. Long since the wall-paper had been replaced by a computer spreadsheet but the name lingered on.

Usually we were given twelve to eighteen months notice of each conference we were to organise, enabling us to select with care the choice of conference centre or hotel. If left any later, one had Hobson's choice, all the best venues would be snapped up by competitors, a scenario which did not fit in with Shorts corporate identity. The aim was to give each operator five or six conferences a year so one conference overlapped several others, all at different stages in the planning. I knew the next conference I was to attend was to be in the Lake District, it was for 35 people. I had already booked the hotel near Ambleside and had worked out speakers, food, transport and jaunts in the afternoon. My task now was to check everything again and in particular to make sure that the senior staff among the delegates were allocated the better rooms. Get that one point wrong, give a junior employee a suite and a manager, a cubby hole and it was very unlikely the client would ever employ Shorts again.

On the wall-paper chart, my name was entered at the bottom of the list and within a short while, I was told that a small group of 20 delegates wanted a venue, not too expensive, within an hour of London for four days, three nights. This was to be a hard working group, not a treat for those employees who had done well, so the countryside was irrelevant, a three-star hotel would be ideal, preferably with access to a gym, though not necessarily in the hotel itself.

It didn't take me more than half a millisecond to realise that the Bull in Hitchin would be the ideal place but as I had a pertinent interest being the proprietor of the establishment, I had to secure clearance from both my bosses and the client who was sending the delegates. This did not prove so much of a hurdle, for in so far as my bosses were concerned, if there were any unsatisfactory complaints, I would have to deal with them and as far as the client was concerned, the price was right.

Once the venue had, in principal, been agreed with the hierarchy I telephoned Martin Lynch my manager, who kindly agreed that if we could come to terms, I would be able to hold a conference in my hotel; he left me in no doubt that he was, in this respect, the manager and my proprietorial interest was an irrelevance. However he did promise to hold the proposed dates open, promised to work out some figures and menus and to come back to me within the fortnight. Martin had agreed to organise access to a local gym of which there were several.

The proposal was then left in abeyance save I did explore two other possible hotels in case the Bull could not after all accommodate the small conference on the right terms. I did not want to be left high and dry or at Martin's mercy.

The Lake District conference proved much harder work than the Italian Job even though there were far fewer delegates. I joined everyone at breakfast, that was fine, and we lunched together after they had worked all morning. In the afternoon I organised a fell walk. On the first day, around Grasmere and on the second day, a little more adventurously, to the Great Gable which I had not seen since my camping days. Each afternoon we had a different walk and I accompanied them all. In the evening, the delegates turned their back on pleasure, and set to working again but this time, in the company of a bottle or two of wine. Each afternoon it rained, sometimes just a drizzle but on one afternoon in particular, it poured. Yet no one cried off, we dressed up in waterproofs and made the best of it. Even in a downpour the Lake District is enchanting and there are numerous low level walks.

Unfortunately when we drove to Coniston the Old Man of Coniston, the local mountain of repute, was not visible but I was far from certain whether it is visible from the village even on a clear day. At least the delegates were a great bunch, there was a lot of laughter, indeed the more it rained and the wetter we all became and we certainly did get wet, the higher our spirits seemed to rise perhaps due in no small measure to the passing round of various hip flasks; the worse the weather the more frequent were the hip flasks rotated. We became a very friendly troop, and they appreciated the work I had put in to organise everything for them.

My original negotiations with Martin, him for the hotel and me for Shorts, proved an interesting experience. I hadn't realised how astute he was, at least, how astute he could be with me and I had not realised how determined I could be in one respect, against my own interests. It was curious how one can fight for a corner even though it is not necessarily the corner that benefits directly, a bit like a teetotaller barrister defending a drunken driver.

'Martin, it's me Lucy,' I said.

'Well you are a stranger. I thought you had all but forgotten us, it must be over a month since you have called.'

'Yes, I have been remiss. Are things well with you.'

'Things are well with me, and what's even more important, things are well with the hotel but I would like to talk to you about some much needed improvements.'

'Improvements to you or to the hotel.'

'I'm virtually perfect,' he said immodestly.

'A bit like Mary Poppins?'

'No, not even a bit like Mary Poppins. It is the hotel that needs some loving care and attention.'

'I have a proposal. I will try to meet up with you, but I am being worked hard at the moment. I want to hold a week long conference at the Bull, and try to secure a portion of that market.'

'I'm listening.'

'To get on the conference circuit we need to refurbish the bedrooms that haven't yet been done up and update the public rooms.'

'How many guests would attend the conference?'

'Thirty to forty. The Bull isn't really big enough to accommodate anything bigger. We might need to screen off some of the ballroom so it looks a bit more cosy. One other point, we will need to offer access to a gym in the evenings. Naturally the people attending the conference will require the best rooms and would like a discount.'

'There will be problems, for example, the regulars will be put out if they have to pay the full price for poorer rooms and may not come back.'

'All the rooms will be lovely, it's just that some will be a little bigger. I am sure all will be most acceptable.'

Eventually terms were agreed, and they were very similar terms to those initially proposed but no doubt honours were done somewhere along the line. The best rooms were reserved for the conference and we agreed that the Bull, which really meant me, would bring forward the refurbishment of the remainder of the bedrooms partly in an effort to impress. The whole of the ground floor and first and second floors were to be made wheelchair accessible. The saloon bar, which I had never been very happy with, would also be redesigned. My parents, bless them, had had a red carpet with a cream design woven into it laid in the saloon, grey orange curtains and very modern lights contrasting sharply with the antique furniture. The whole didn't gel to my mind. I thought we could keep the red carpet as it was still in very good condition and it was the most expensive item to change after the furniture. The curtains I changed to a cream, matching the cream in the carpet pattern, but with Cambridge blue added as a motif. For the upholstery I chose Cambridge blue with a cream pattern woven into it. The pictures, prints actually, were all replaced as were the lights.

I have great difficulty choosing light fittings. The choice is by necessity, restricted to what is available in the warehouse or catalogue and trying to picture lights in a warehouse, transferred to ones own walls is not easy and once installed it is even less easy to change them. Fortunately a friend is a most competent draftswoman; I asked her to sketch the saloon as it was and as it would be with the proposed alterations, it is much simpler to change a drawing.

As an additional expenditure I bought new uniforms for the staff and changed the pillows for all of the bedrooms. I have a personal hatred of old hotel pillows. Pillows get heavier with prolonged usage, very few hotels ever get them cleaned; accordingly the heavier the pillows are the less hygienic they are as they become full of debris, human debris. There are some very heavy pillows in some of the hotels I have visited. The object of these various improvements at the Bull was not to increase the number of stars the Bull has allocated to it, from three stars to four stars, but rather to make the hotel more attractive so that the occupancy rate might rise from the present fairly low 63 per cent. Increasing the star rating would have been very difficult for the Bull, a small hotel of great age. One way of increasing occupancy rating was to attract small conferences during the week and wedding receptions at weekends, the improvements were all designed towards that end. As can be imagined my telephone conversations with Martin proved very lengthy and numerous, he wasn't opposing my ideas at all, indeed they largely reflected what he had wanted to do for quite some time, he would have liked to have gone further but it was not he who was the one who had to sign the loan agreements for the finance.

Gratifyingly the conference at the Bull was very successful. It was very different indeed from my previous conferences I had organised recently, especially the one in Sorrento. In Hitchin the delegates started work immediately after an early breakfast and with only a short lunch break worked continuously until after 6 o'clock. Apart from accommodation and access to the gym little else was expected from the Bull save for a quite spectacular supper, this being a specific request of the client. My chef surpassed himself, each evening producing a masterpiece. It was on the last day of the conference that fate took a twist. As a break with being too formal I was wearing a pair of white slacks with a chocolate brown knitted sweater both which I had bought in Milan. The sweater had tight sleeves, flaring at the wrists, a cut away neck and buttons up the front. The delegates were leaving by taxi to travel to the station on the first leg of the short journey back to London, and I, in the lobby as usual was the last to leave, checking everything, saying goodbye, helping Gloria with the bar bills, answering the telephone, sorting things out. By 10 o'clock peace reigned, relative peace, the vacuum cleaners could be heard everywhere.

'Were we successful?' asked Gloria, she knew that the conference was important to the future of the hotel.

'You certainly were,' I said, 'and what's even better is that we should be able to attract several conferences a year. There are quite a few firms who want to get work done, rather than have a conference in a magical playground. Where firms want a good working atmosphere rather than a treat for the delegates, the Bull scores highly; much cheaper than London. Hitchin is near to the Stansted and Luton airports, and has good rail links. When it's not a question of giving the delegates a treat, for being the best salesman for example, the Bull scores well'

'You mean it's not a treat staying at the Bull?' said Gloria.

'T'is for me,' I said, 'But not in quite the same way as

Barbados.'

'I haven't seen much of you since you left Colchester. What have you been up to in London, You have some amazing clothes, look at what you are wearing now, Your suede shoes are to die for, those white trousers they are cut so well, look at that side pocket slightly curved, and that brown cardi. It's so soft and stylish, unlike any other cardigan I've ever seen. It's catwalk stuff. And that outfit you were wearing last night.'

'Oh that old thing,' I said laughing, 'Did you really like it?'

'I bet you didn't buy it in Hitchin.'

'No not in Hitchin, that's true. How are you keeping?'

'Not so bad, mustn't grumble. I get tired but then who doesn't and I keep getting pins and needles in my fingers, Carpal tunnel I think it's called, it tends to keep me awake at night, just part of getting old I suppose. I'm still waiting for an appointment at the Lister Hospital. Oh, talking of Lister Hospital, do you remember Rosemary, she used to work here when your parents were alive.'

'Rosemary Parker, yes, I remember her well, what has she been up to?'

'She had to have a hysterectomy poor dear but it went wrong, she is in a bad way evidently.'

'She cannot be more than thirty-five years old, much too young for a hysterectomy.'

'Not so it seems. I looked in on her yesterday, she was very low, she might appreciate seeing you just for a bit of a chat.'

'I was going to drive straight back to London and get out of Martin's hair but I suppose I could make a detour to the Lister. Do you recall which ward she is in? If I do go, I had better take a present, perhaps some flowers.'

Martin came up, I congratulated him. He looked really pleased.

'Perhaps the first of many conferences,' I said.

'It was a lot of extra work,' he said meaningfully.

'The hotel really looks good,' I said ignoring him, 'The new decor in the saloon bar is a great success, everything went off well, I'm really pleased.'

'Yes, the end result was worth the upheaval but it is always difficult operating a business whilst renovation work is taking place. Nobody likes the smell of oil paint especially when eating or sleeping; it even got the staff down after a while, the smell seemed to creep everywhere. I am glad it's finished. don't the uniforms look good,' said Martin.

'I even managed to sell the old ones.' said Gloria.

'Heavens, who to?'

'A small hotel in Kent. They are just starting up. They were really pleased but I didn't get a fortune for them.'

'Were takings really bad over the last few months?'

'The bars were still busy but the room reservations were down. The real problem lay in the fact that we couldn't hold any large function here, with half of the public rooms out of commission. These functions are the real moneyspinners. That's corrected itself now, and we are fully booked for about the next three months.'

'Thank you, both of you. I had better be getting off to Lister Hospital.'

'You're not ill are you?' asked Martin. He seemed concerned.

'No, no just visiting thankfully. See you soon.'

I don't enjoy hospital visiting but then, who does. I made my way to the hospital car park, then along an endless corridor up to the wards. Putting on my caring smile, I asked the nurse on duty where Rosemary might be found and was shown into a small side ward. There looking forlorn was Rosemary slumped against a pillow. She didn't present a particularly pretty sight, no make up, her hair very much askew and a bit dirty. Rosemary was wearing an indeterminate hospital gown off white in colour, exactly matching the bed clothes and a near match to the colour of her skin. She looked as if she was completely worn out, she had been weeping, her red eyes being the only thing giving any colour at all.

I smiled at her, and proffered my bunch of yellow fuchsias; she offered me a bit of a smile back but made no effort to take the flowers.

'Hello,' I said, 'how are you?'

'I've been better,' she said.

'You poor old thing, what's been going wrong?'

'I had an infection in my womb, I ignored the symptoms for ages and when I did eventually seek help it seems I left it too late, the doctors said I must have a hysterectomy and that was what was performed but something is still very much amiss. This morning they found out that I have some internal bleeding and it seems the surgeons might have discovered some cancer, I'm really frightened.'

'That's horrid! What are they going to do to you next?'

'This evening they are going to try to stop the bleeding, they took a biopsy and we are now waiting for the results of the tests, they should know either later on today or tomorrow. I feel morally, spiritually, metaphorically and physically gutted. I'm frightened, tired and keep crying, everything is bloody awful, I cannot think how it could get worse.'

We chatted for a little while, I am not sure if my presence was a help to her or not, I tried to comfort her but she kept saying that she thought she was going to die and I suppose it might have been true. I started to tell her what I had been doing but then stopped as she seemed only to compare her plight with my lifestyle: after only about twenty minutes, I made my excuses and got up to go.

'Before you go,' she said 'I have something to tell you.' Then she mumbled something I could not quite catch.

'Say again,' I said.

She gave a gulp, and said a bit louder 'It was me, I killed that man in your hotel.'

'I killed Richard Jenkins,' said Rosemary, 'but I didn't mean to.'

I sat down again by her bedside, very bewildered.

'What's all this about?' I asked.

'I'll deny I said anything to you if you tell on me?'

'What's all this about?' I repeated.

'I've been wondering who I could tell. Most of the people I know aren't very good at keeping a secret. I have to tell someone in case the police make an arrest after I, well, just in case the operation isn't successful, I couldn't have that on my conscience as well, I couldn't have someone rotting in jail for a crime I committed.'

'Rosemary, please start from the beginning. What are you trying to tell me?'

'I meant to really hurt that wretched Jeffrey Barrett, I tried to give him some wine I had put some stuff in but instead it seems I delivered it to the wrong room, Richard Jenkins drunk it and he died and I didn't mean him to die. I didn't mean anyone to die. I still don't understand how the wrong person drunk the wine, I checked so carefully on the hotel computer.'

'Why did you want to hurt Jeffrey Barrett?'

'He was supplying drugs to my son, and the drugs just about destroyed him altogether. Barrett, he's sneaky, he starts off giving kids drugs free of charge, then when they are hooked, starts giving them hard drugs and really starts to charge. Kevin is on heroin, he's a shadow of what he used to be like, he used to be fun, he's not any more; he doesn't wash properly, he is totally self centred it's pitiful, he's destroyed my son's life. I'd like another go at flipping high and mighty Jeff Barrett,'

'How do you know it was Mr Barrett who supplied the drugs?'

'Kevin had a long chat with me, he explained what had gone wrong. Usually he doesn't talk sense but this time I caught him on the right balance. He said it was Barrett who started him off,' said Rosemary.

'Tell me what you did,' I said.

'Why do you need to know any more?'

'Because nobody will believe me if I don't have some proof. I can't just say it was Rosemary who did it but you can't ask her now.'

'You won't be able to catch me out.'

'Tell me anyway,' I said.

'During the time folk take drugs, they go through a variety of stages. They can be amazingly aggressive, they can be fairly normal. They can be very quiet or they can be a bit chatty. I asked him how he started to take drugs, not as an aggressive stance but just chatting, I had to treat him with kid gloves, it was really difficult. If I seemed to be pressing he would just clam up. God I am tired.'

'Do you want a rest, shall I come back in an hour or so?'

I asked.

'Kevin told me that he was given drugs, just handed them when he was drinking in one of the Hitchin pubs, this happened on several occasions, he didn't tell me how many or what they were. It just got worse and worse from there, he went down hill quickly. He kept blaming Jeffrey Barrett. The name didn't mean anything to me at that time but I was in the Bull's reception area chatting to Ian whose family I have known for years, when I heard Ian answer the 'phone to a Jeffrey Barrett. I just put two and two together, there couldn't be two people with that name in Hitchin. I thought that if I made him really ill, he might realise what he was doing to other people,' said Rosemary, in fits and starts and between bouts of crying.

'You thought he might be remorseful,' I said.

'Did I. Well the long and the short of it is that I went off to the library and found a book on dangerous plants. Hitchin has a long connection with growing plants for chemist shops in days gone by and there are lots of books, someone gave their collection to the town I think. I got together as many bits of poisonous plants as I could find, bits of yew, bits of laburnum trees, oh I don't know what else. I put them all into a jar with a small amount of hot water and shook it up, left it for a couple of days, then the mixture went into a juice extractor. Eventually a dribble or two of a liquid was produced which I hoped would be enough to make Barrett unwell. I put my concoction into a bottle of wine I bought in the supermarket, I made sure it was red wine so any slight change of colour wouldn't be noticed. I put on one of the hotel's spare uniforms and took the bottle on a tray up to his room, that was the easy bit for me, I know the Bull as well as you do, I worked there for six years full time.'

'Was it six years that you were there.'

'But the wrong person got poisoned, and he died. I didn't mean to kill anyone,' Rosemary started to cry again.

'Ian muddled up the room keys, you took the drink to Richard Jenkin's room, he drank it and it certainly didn't agree with him. For a long time we were looking for a person with a grudge against Richard Jenkins.' Rosemary started to cry again, eventually a nurse came and waived me away.

I was very thoughtful as I left Rosemary's bedside, it seemed a good idea to have another word with Jeffrey Barrett as soon as might be possible. I walked into the main ward, then made my way to the exit which opened out onto a wide landing where the lift shafts were situated. Other wards opened onto this landing as well, there was a large window, and by the window a telephone. I dialled Hitchin Police Station and somewhat to my surprise was put through to D.C.I. Blake almost immediately. He had not forgotten me.

'Miss White, what can I do for you?'

'Hello, Inspector, I would like to speak to Jeffrey Barrett again and wonder if you can put me in touch?'

'I can't help at all?'

'I think I should talk to him first. Are you in contact with him?'

'Do you mean you want to talk to him on the telephone or in person?'

'In person if possible.'

'Just a minute.'

I held on for what seemed an age. At last the Inspector's voice came down the line.

'I cannot get hold of him but it has been suggested that if you were in your bar at the Bull tonight, at say 7 o'clock, he might be able to drop in but then again, he might not. That's the best I can do for you at the moment.'

'Thank you kindly.'

'Are you sure that there is nothing you can tell me.'

'Perhaps later.' I rang off and stood looking out of the window realising that I was gazing at the farmland over which I used to ride MacTell and Archie. It looked very different from high up and I spent several minutes trying to get my bearings. I had not seen the horses nor Caroline for such a long time, I had several hours to kill before I my appointment, if that's what it was, with Mr Barrett so I decided to call in the stables on my way back to Hitchin. At least the horses would be there. Before I left the hospital I thought I had better reserve a room at the Bull for the night. It had been a long time since I had occupied Room 413 on a semi permanent basis, I had been using a guest room all week and I might as well stay the extra night and drive back early Saturday morning when the traffic would be freer. Driving back towards Hitchin I passed under the motorway and made my way along the familiar country lanes to Todds Green, the court shoes I was wearing were hardly suitable to explore stables and a yard, perhaps Caroline could lend me a pair of wellies.

It had been over a year since I last visited the stable yard. Caroline's Audi was parked in the driveway but so was Charles's old van, a complication I had not envisaged, my impromptu visit had coincided with his call. I had not seen, nor had I had any contact with Charles since our heated discussion at Colchester, it all seemed so long ago now. I was in two minds whether to simply drive away but realised that I had been spotted. Retreat was not an option.

I parked my impeccable silver Merc next to Charles's old van wishing the contrast wasn't quite so acute and walked over to where the horses were tethered. Patting MacTell and playing with his forelock I heard Charles say:

'Oh, it's you!'

'Yes it's me,' I said. Why was I nervous.

'Aren't you a bit overdressed for the Countryside?' he said, then turned his back on me and carried on with his work. Not much of a greeting, he certainly didn't give the impression of wanting me to stay, feeling very much in the way, I mumbled goodbye and made for my car intending to drive away but it was not to be. Caroline had spotted me from her kitchen window, had walked out to greet me, we kissed cheeks or to be more precise, kissed the air one inch away from our cheeks. She beamed at me, grabbed me by the arm and said I was staying for a cup of tea. She also grabbed Charles by the arm and said he was joining us and led us into her house ignoring Charles's protestations that he was too busy.

'Don't be silly you need a break,' she said to Charles and to me, 'My word you do look good.'

'I was on my way back to London when I was diverted to Lister Hospital and popped in here on the off chance as I hadn't seen you for ages,' I said.

'Are you unwell?' asked Charles. Heavens, a spark of human interest, I thought.

'No, it wasn't me that was ill, I was visiting a chum who has had a rough time.'

'Did you know Lucy was coming here today?' Charles asked Caroline. He sounded very suspicious.

'I haven't seen, spoken to or heard from Lucy for months,' said Caroline offering Charles and me a piece of bread, a slice of cheese and some jam, a Danish custom she had picked up from somewhere, Denmark I suppose. 'What's eating you two?'

Charles, helping himself to a slice of bread said nothing. I decided it was time to pay my dues as a guest and make polite conversation.

'How are the horses?' I asked nobody in particular.

'I thought Archie had a bad tooth so I telephoned Charles this morning,' said Caroline and indeed Caroline's address book lay open just by the telephone, open at the letter 'D'. I watched Charles gaze idly at it.

'I see I'm under 'D' presumably 'D' for done with,' said Charles acidly, he reached for the book, 'And whilst that is still my telephone number, I moved from that address about four years ago.' He picked up a pen and entered his correct address, crossing out the old one with a little too much force.

'It's the address you gave me,' said Caroline.

'I am sure it was four years ago but I haven't lived there for ages.'

'I always telephone you, I never have written. Just as well it seems.' said Caroline.

'I wrote to you,' I said to Charles.

'When?'

'Ages ago now, just after ... well just after.'

'I didn't get any letter from you.'

'Don't you remember Caroline, I telephoned you for Charles's address.'

'To be honest I don't, I was probably doing three things at once but if you asked me for Charles address, that's the one I would have given you,' said Caroline nodding to the address book.

'The old one in the address book?'

'Yes of course.'

'Ah!' I said.

'Ah!' said Charles.

'What does ah mean? asked Caroline.

'It means a lack of communication,' said Charles.

'Important?' asked Caroline.

'I don't suppose so now.' I said to Caroline, and to Charles I said 'Wouldn't a letter sent to your old address still have reached you?'

'It was some digs I was in about four years ago. I don't suppose the landlady still has my address to forward letters on even if she remembered who I was.'

'Ah,' I said.

'Wouldn't the sender of a letter put his or her name on the back of the envelope or the top of the letter?'

'Yes, but probably only the town and the Christian name.'

'Ah,' said Charles.

'Stimulating conversation,' said Caroline who is usually ahead of the game, 'Do I detect an undercurrent here?'

'What would this letter have said?' asked Charles.

'Probably apologetic in tone,' I said.

'I have just remembered I may have left the iron upstairs,' said Caroline and made a political exit which was kind of her.

'I wrote a letter to you after our row last time we met,' I said, 'Apologising for jumping to conclusions, just said I was very sorry and things like that. I never dreamt that you didn't get the letter.'

'These things happen,' said Charles.

'Would it have made any difference if you had received my letter?' I asked.

'It might have done.'

'Pity we can't turn the clock back,' I said. I was really nervous, why was I nervous. 'Perhaps we could meet for a drink, just for a chat?'

'You're all posh now, you won't want to be seen with me.'

'6 o'clock at the Bull,' I said.

Charles looked at me, I was not sure if he nodded or not, I just couldn't tell, he picked up his mug of tea, drank it down, said 'I really must get on' and walked out of the kitchen. Caroline must have heard him go for she appeared a few moments later and looked at me quizzingly, I just shrugged, so we started to chat about her children. After only a few minutes we heard Charles's van start up and drive off. I wondered if it would be the last time I would see him.

I left Caroline's friendly kitchen and drove to the Bull which I must say was equally friendly in a more reserved way, everyone there was surprised to see me back but made no comment. They gave me Room 26, I hadn't slept in there before but I thought it wasn't a bad idea to lay a ghost, it was 5.15 pm. I found myself with nothing much to do for three quarters of an hour until 6 o'clock, when I might or might not meet Charles and the time did pass slowly. I switched on the television, on one programme it was wall to wall cartoons, and I have never liked cartoons apart from the Simpsons and some of the Walt Disney films. The local news was on the second channel, that didn't interest me nor did an American Golf Tournament on the third. I decided to write a short note explaining what I had been told by Rosemary.

Writing the note took only a few minutes and when that was done I sat watching the clock, gradually the hand climbed up towards the hour, so I wandered down to the bar just in case Charles came, this was not the time to be late. I walked into the bar and sat at a table, this was also not the occasion to be serving the drinks or washing up. If Charles came, I had to give him my full attention. I could see the staff on duty behind the bar eyeing me obviously wondering what I was doing relaxing in the public areas, an unusual occupation for me, even when not on duty I would never just sit in the saloon bar. I waited and waited, I kept reminding myself that the hotel kept all of its clocks six minutes fast to help when closing time came. I wondered why I was feeling so nervous, like someone on their first date, perhaps the butterfly feeling never really goes away. Charles came, the object of my nervous tension, he walked over to my table and asked me if he could get me a drink.

Charles must have known that a nod from me would bring at least two of my bar staff over, they were all watching me albeit out of the corner of their eyes but getting drinks served in that way evidently wasn't how Charles had decided things were going to be done that evening. I asked for a sprizza. Needless to say he was served instantly even through he was not necessarily the first in the queue. Charles came back with a tray and a packet of crisps. I wasn't at all sure whether he was angry with me, conciliatory, inquisitive or argumentative, no doubt the next fifteen minutes would make things clear. He sat down at my table and looked at me.

'Hello,' I said neutrally.

'I'm not sure why I'm here,' said Charles.

I ignored the heavy inference and asked him what he had been doing.

'I went skiing with some friends between Christmas and New Year,' he said 'apart from that, lots of work, a few drinks. I still live in the same house, drive the same van, see the same horses. It probably sounds very boring to someone with your lifestyle but I enjoy it. It suits. I don't particularly yearn for a flash car or flash friends, I am quite a happy contented person.'

'Tell me about skiing?'

'I went to Austria, to the small village of Scheffan with two friends. It is really picturesque, we skied for much of the day stopping for lunch and coffee breaks. There were bars set high on the hills overlooking the slopes. Among other things they served hot wine with spices mixed in with some spirits, my word ones skiing did improve after having two of those.'

Suddenly his enthusiasm showed through and it was the Charles I had fallen in love with. We talked about inconsequential things, work, skiing, sport, alterations to the Bull. I had to keep an eye on the time and had not appreciated that Charles realised I was doing this.

'If you are in a rush to go, then that's fine,' he said a little testily.

'No it's not that at all, I have to meet someone at 7 o'clock. Would you have supper with me please?'

'Not at the Bull.' It was a statement not a question and it meant an acceptance. He could easily have made an excuse to go. 'And please don't wear those clothes, you stand out a bit too much in Hitchin, tonight at least, make it frumpy.'

'You choose where we should eat,' I said, and he did.

The time for my meeting with Jeffrey Barrett was drawing near, I thanked Charles for the drink, we had only had the one and stood up. Our table was immediately claimed by another couple, it was very noisy, the couple came between us and we drifted apart but at least we had arranged to meet later that evening. I stood around not quite knowing what to do, so started collecting up dirty beer glasses from around the bar and taking them over to the serving counter, a reflex action really, I had done it so often before. I wasn't dressed to wash them up, after a little while Jeffrey Barrett was at my side.

'Can we talk somewhere quiet?' he said. I slipped him the key to Room 26.

'I will meet you there in five minutes,' I said. He went away unobtrusively and I followed him shortly afterwards.

I climbed the stairs, knocked on the closed door which I had expected to find open. He let me in and I saw that his face was very troubled.

'Someone has been trying to find me today,' he said.

'Yes it was me.'

'I mean apart from yourself, I don't know who it is but I am being a bit more careful than I usually bother to be. There is a trial due to start on Thursday at the Old Bailey in London and I am a key witness. I am a bit vulnerable until this is all over, what did you want to say to me?'

'I know the name of the person who tried to kill you, and indeed did kill Richard Jenkins.'

'You do, what's his name?'

'She, and it is a she, is out of action for a few days but she is intent on trying again.'

'Who is it.'

'There's a problem there, naming names. As soon as I tell you, you are bound to tell D.C.I. Blake who is bound to approach her and arrest her. Once I have started the ball rolling, nobody can stop it.'

'This is the classic case of one person knowing something vital and that person getting killed to stop her telling.'

'That's why we are having this meeting. Please humour me just for a moment or two. I have written the name on a piece of paper with a short explanation and have posted this off by second class post. If I do not contact the person I sent it to, they will telephone D.C.I. Blake on Monday morning.'

'Go on then.'

'This person, the murderer, said she wanted to hurt you not Richard Jenkins.'

'Yes, go on.'

'She thinks that you have been trading in drugs and has made a junkie out of someone she loves.'

'I never did.'

'So let's work out a plan to prove that you didn't and she

will stop being a danger to you. Once she has stopped being a danger you will be safer. You are not a policeman, you are a security agent whatever that is, you can decide whereas D.C.I. Plod cannot.'

'Who is D.C.I. Plod?'

'Oh yes, that was Charles's pet name for D.C.I. Blake and it stuck.'

'I understand what you are saying, but don't necessarily agree with it, what's your plan?'

'I don't know how you operate, or why she should think that you are responsible, that's why we needed to meet. How much can you tell me?'

'I'll think about it, meanwhile would you help me.'

'I'll do anything I can.'

'Would you let me stay here the night, obviously I will pay, but after last time I don't want my name in your computer.'

'You mean you want to pay me money to sleep with me.'

'Not sexually no, heavens above that's not what I am suggesting at all. This is an hotel, I need somewhere to sleep tonight and am not keen on going back to my hotel room in case I am followed again.'

'Are you really in danger?'

'I rather think I might be.'

'Very well, you can use this room, at least its twin bedded, I may or may not sleep here. What about food.'

'Well I haven't eaten.'

'I'll get a tray from the kitchen and say it's for me.'

I caught sight of my reflection in the mirror. I suppose I did look a bit dressed up having changed for Charles into cream linen trousers, a turquoise silk top and a long waist coat, great for Islington but for Hitchin, maybe not. The cream trousers would pass, I put on some brown sandals which incidentally cost a fortune but didn't look it, it was what to wear on top that caused me problems. I had nothing frumpy.

I looked at Jeffrey Barrett, 'Could I possibly borrow your jumper?' I asked.

'What?'

'Your jumper, may I borrow it please.'

'But I need it.'

'I need to look frumpy, it really is important to me. All the clothes I have bought down from London are too exclusive for tonight and your jumper is just the thing. You can stay in my hotel, free of charge and have some supper, if I can borrow your jumper.'

Looking very doubtful indeed, he took off the garment and handed it to me.

'Thanks.' I said, 'but I'll get your supper before putting it on.'

In the kitchen I made up a tray of food from bits lying in the fridge, a large piece of Camembert cheese, a portion of cold chicken, some bread and pickle, a helping of sherry trifle, ostentatiously it was for myself nobody queried why I wanted to eat alone but then they wouldn't. I had been very sociable with the delegates over the last few nights and it was natural that I would like a bit of a change. I picked up a couple of bottles of beer and took them all upstairs making sure that I wasn't followed.

Jeffrey Barrett was standing in the room by the window. 'Food!' I said, 'And drink.'

'I need a few things from my room at the Red Lion where I had booked in for the night. If I gave you the key, would you kindly pick them up for me?'

'Gladly,' I said. 'Meanwhile have you thought how we can satisfy this person that you are honourable?'

'Probably,' he said 'but I am still thinking, give me a couple of hours. Thank you for the meal.'

I nodded, pulled his jumper over my head, brushed my hair, touched up my make-up and left the room to meet Charles at a Chinese restaurant just round the corner for a meal. I walked down the stairs making a note of anything worth making a note about, but there was nothing. I walked out of the Bull and made my way towards Brand Street walking across the Old Market Square looking quite enchanting, the square, not me, I must have looked very frumpy but that is what Charles had requested. In fact he crossed my path, I had not seen him approach me, he seemed cross.

'I didn't see you there,' I said smiling.

'I nearly didn't come,' he said, 'I saw you wondering off with that man, I expect you went to a bedroom with him, and now you come back wearing his clothes.'

I stopped walking, my heart sunk, I couldn't believe it, it was history repeating itself.

'We can't have these misunderstandings between us. I turned to face Charles, you wanted me frumpy, I'm as frumpy as I can get but I had to borrow his jumper, I care deeply for you, I haven't gone off with anyone else, damn it I didn't, that was only Jeffrey Barrett, I.. I..' but he didn't let me finish.

'Just winding you up and getting my own back. A bit of trust from now on,' said Charles.

'Oh yes please,' I said.

'Let's eat then.'

'I fancy some seaweed.'

'Is that to eat or roll in?' he asked trying to make a joke.

'And then perhaps prawns in black bean sauce with green peppers. What do you fancy?'

'As its quite dark, I think I might fancy you, are you as pretty in daylight?'

We walked, surprisingly, hand in hand past Boots and Woolworths, Barclays Bank and the Bakers, turned a corner, and climbed the stairs, for the restaurant was on the first floor. We were shown to a table. We looked at the menu and looked at the wine on offer, although it did not mean that much to me, I did see that they had a bottle of the Cotes-du-Rhone 1993.

'Charles, look, that's the same wine which was delivered to Richard Jenkins with the poison in it. I had a long chat with

Martin about the difference in quality between the various years. I should really like to get the two bottles together and see if I can tell the difference, Martin said they were like chalk and cheese but he is a bit of a wine buff. Let's buy a bottle to take away with us and see if we can tell which is which just to taste.'

So as well as ordering the drinks with the meal, we bought an unopened bottle of the Cotes-du-Rhone 1993, I thought it might be rather fun to give Martin a blind testing to see if he really could tell the difference between the two years or whether it was all talk.

Over our meal we chatted about this and that, caught up with what we had been doing, and what we wanted to be doing. I decided to tell Charles everything I knew about the murderer, the murder, Rosemary and Jeffrey Barrett, I didn't want any more misunderstandings, no more secrets between us. Charles wasn't very keen on me sharing a room with Jeffrey Barrett for the night, whether it was because he wanted me to himself or because he was worried Jeffrey Barrett would become amorous I could not tell; perhaps neither. Towards the end of the meal I explained that I had to pop into the Red Lion to pick up some things for Jeffrey Barrett, kindly Charles said he would come too.

We both knew the public rooms of the Red Lion quite well, but neither of us had ever been up to any of the bedrooms. I took the key Jeffrey Barrett had given me, out of my handbag, it wasn't a proper key in the sense of a key made from a length of steel, rather it was a plastic card which was, I gather, fairly easy to replace if guests ran off with it. We trudged up the stairs, there wasn't a lift, pressing light buttons on as we went, they were all on time switches and the timers didn't give you long before turning themselves off, putting the staircase in darkness again. We reached the door of Jeffrey Barrett's room but nothing happened when we put the card into the slot and then withdrew it. We tried several times but the door would not open until we realised that timing was everything and that we were doing it far too quickly. Slowly we put the card in, counted to four, slowly we withdrew the card again, then three things happened almost simultaneously.

The door opened swinging back on its hinges, the timer on the light switch in the corridor turned the lights off plunging us into darkness and an explosion occurred. Someone had fired a shot at us, and we were hit.

Charles had been shot but I didn't know it until quite a long time afterwards, when I could piece things together. All I knew at the time, was that there was a flash, and then a very loud bang, followed by another and another then I heard Charles groaning, it seems we both sunk to the floor. What was even more terrible was that whoever was firing, kept on firing, it seemed as if all hell was let loose. Thankfully we were now protected to some extent from being hit again by the height of the bed which we were crouching behind. The bullets flew safely over our heads and embedded themselves in the timber work behind us. Charles was still groaning, there were no lights on but I could hear someone shouting from downstairs. In all of this turmoil I became crosser and crosser, I became incensed that anyone should treat us in this manner. I suppose I also became protective of Charles but I didn't stop to analyse my thoughts, I just hurled, with all my force, the bottle of Cotes du Rhone I was still holding, in a wide arc around my head and let it fly in the direction of the shooting but a little higher. The firing stopped, there was a thud and for a moment or two silence. Then footsteps running, groaning, yelling, screaming. The screaming was me.

Suddenly the landing light came on, then the room light. I was covered in blood and so was Charles who now lay on the floor, I couldn't see anything else as the side of the bed blocked my view of the rest of the room. I tried to move Charles but only succeeded in making him scream, he was clutching at his leg and seemed to have been shot three or four times but I couldn't really tell, more people came into the room, I have no idea who they were but they weren't in uniform. I remember voices around me everyone kept asking what had happened and then after what seemed to be a very long time, the police came. As I wasn't hurt, only frightened and dazed, they half carried me down some stairs and put me into another bedroom, a policeman stayed with me and kept asking me questions.

'I need to know your name please,' he said.

'What, oh yes, it's Lucy White.'

'I also need to know the name of the person who fired at you.'

'I don't know, please tell me how Charles is.'

'Is that the person who was shot?'

'Yes, Charles, Charles Duggan, how is he please?

'I am afraid I don't know, I understand that he's going to be taken to Lister Hospital. This is a very serious matter Miss, why did that man shoot at both of you?'

'Truly, I don't know. We just entered the room and someone fired the gun. I haven't even seen the man's face.'

'But why would he be waiting to shoot you in your room?'

'It's not our room, we were just collecting things, the room is booked out in the name of Jeffrey Barrett.'

'Where is this Mr Jeffrey Barrett?'

'He's in his room at my hotel, the Bull. Would you please

telephone the Lister Hospital for me.'

'It's much too early to do that Miss. Why should Mr Barrett have a room here and also a room at the Bull?'

'I really think you should be asking Mr Barrett these questions.'

'We will but he isn't here, you must have some idea of what went on. Why should Mr Barrett reserve this room, and also a room at the Bull?'

'I think he just changed his mind.'

'So you don't know who shot you or why or why he should lie in wait or why Mr Barrett books into two hotel rooms for the same night in the same town?'

'I assume that the man was waiting for Mr Barrett and we just happened along, it was very dark. I threw a bottle of wine into the air and presumably hit whoever it was as the shooting stopped'

'Why would ...'

We were going round in circles, it seemed that this uniformed officer had not been informed of Jeffrey Barrett's undercover work, and it didn't seem my place to enlighten him but it made my story sound very implausible; the explanation fell far short of what the policeman considered to be satisfactory. Fortunately at that moment he was interrupted by a sharp rap on the door.

'Who's there?' asked the constable.

'D.C.I. Blake, please let me in.'

'Thank goodness,' I said, or did I just think it. The

constable opened the door, and the inspector entered the room. He took one look at who I was, obviously recognising me, heard that the room had been booked under the name of Jeffrey Barrett and sent the constable off on other duties. Evidently the inspector had already been up to the scene of the shooting, had seen Charles but did not know his name and had never seen him before.

There were just the two of us present in the room, it was quiet, I felt reassured by his presence but started to shake uncontrollably and then felt sick. I had to make a dash for the bathroom and it was ten or fifteen minutes before I could make a reappearance. The inspector was waiting for me patiently. I returned to the room and sat down on the bed. I felt awful.

I told D.C.I. Blake all that I knew.

'This Charles,' he said. 'Is he your young man?'

'I hope so, but our evening was cut short.'

'I really must try to get in touch with Jeffrey Barrett. I wonder where he is now.'

'Oh he's at the Bull.'

'Then it would be a sensible course to go to see him,' said D.C.I. Blake, he left me for a few moments, went upstairs, and returned without saying anything to me.

'Incidentally Mr Barrett doesn't want anyone to know where he is tonight,' I said. 'He told me that someone had been trying to find him today and it worried him.'

'Yes, you.'

'Apart from me.'

Nodding, D.C.I. Blake took off his jacket and tie so that he was a bit less formal I suppose and walked me out of the rear entrance of the Red Lion and by a devious route, to the rear entrance of the Bull. We climbed the stairs together and knocked on the door of Room 26. An eye appeared in the spy hole, the door opened and we walked into tranquillity.

Whilst D.C.I. Blake brought Jeffrey Barrett up to date with the events of the previous hour, I showered and changed, throwing away all the clothes that I had been wearing. I walked back into the room and tried to telephone the hospital but was told that as I was not a relative, they could not talk to me. They asked me if Charles was my boyfriend and all I could say was that I didn't know which sounded pathetic but I daren't have a nurse tell Charles that his girlfriend had enquired after him, in case I wasn't. In the end I insisted that D.C.I. Blake telephoned the hospital, he was told by the ward sister it was too soon to know anything.

I had to tell my story again for the benefit of Jeffrey Barrett, both men asked me questions, I knew few of the answers. In due course they both went out of the room and eventually I fell asleep and slept for the rest of the night.

Waking early, I dressed hurriedly and drove a little too quickly to the Lister Hospital, I went to the men's surgical ward which appeared to be deserted. I hunted round for Charles's bed, but could I find it, I could not. I didn't know the layout of the wards but there seemed to be beds everywhere, most of them empty, presumably because it was the weekend. I searched around and realised there appeared to be four main wards at one end and four at the other a bit like a bell bar. Off the centre of the bell bar was the nurses station and various side wards, eventually I saw Charles in one of these, although at first I didn't recognise him, he had tubes and things everywhere. I let myself into the room but there was no sign of life from the sleeping bundle and after sitting there for about twenty minutes. I slipped out again unnoticed. I thought of going to have a look to see how Rosemary was getting on but I found her bed was empty, there was not much I could do for a while. I left the hospital and popped into an eating place almost next door where they were serving travellers with breakfast. Over orange juice, coffee, poached eggs on toast and a glass of water I tried to read the newspapers which I usually found a delight but they could not hold my attention that morning, I found it difficult to concentrate. The food was OK without any sparkle or perhaps I just wasn't in the mood for eating; I kept wondering what was happening.

It was a bit like Prokofiev's Peter and the Wolf. Charles was in one room, unable to leave it because of all of the tubes, the person who shot at us was in another with a police guard, Rosemary was now no doubt in a third room after her operation. I alone it seemed, could wander around freely, but could not get any response from any people in any of the rooms, I personified the wolf but did not feel predatory. I breakfasted slowly but after fifty minutes felt I had to leave the table, so made my way back to the wards in the hospital, through the double doors, past reception, along the corridor, up in the lifts first to Rosemary's ward, where a nurse was just leaving her bedside.

'How is she?' I asked.

'She's doing fine. She had her second operation last night and is recovering well, but at present she is still asleep, I think we should leave her for a bit.'

I walked on, up to our mysterious gunman's room. There was still a policeman outside his door.

'Good morning,' I said .

'Hello Miss, did you want something?'

'I'm one of the people he shot at last night.' I said, 'Do you know who he is?'

'Can't really say Miss.'

'Can I see him?'

'No best not to Miss.'

I wandered off to Charles's ward and immediately saw that he was much brighter. He appeared to have washed, shaved, breakfasted and was wide awake.'

'Was it you who came in earlier?' he asked.

'It was indeed.'

'I thought I must have dreamt it.'

'Shall I stay or shall I go?'

'What do you want to do?'

'I'd like to stay please.'

'Good. Sit down and ask me how I feel.'

'How do you feel?'

'Don't ask.'

It was silly but we both laughed, which hurt Charles a little.

'Really how are you?'

'They say that I was lucky. Someone shoots at us out of the blue and they say we are lucky!'

'I think they mean ...'

'Yes, I know what they mean, it could have been much more serious. Happily I am really only grazed, the bullet could have done a great deal of damage. Nobody has yet told me what happened or why?' said Charles.

'I can tell you what happened,' I said. 'Jeffrey Barrett asked us to collect some things for him from his hotel room at the Red Lion, when we opened the door, someone started to fire a gun at us, the bullet hit you in your thigh, we both crumpled to the floor and thankfully were protected by the side of the bed. He kept firing but it was dark so he could not aim properly, I threw a bottle of wine at him and I seemed to have hit him. He was knocked out and was brought here with you in the same ambulance. I cannot however tell you why it all happened, why he choose to fire the gun at us or who he is. We were really fortunate that the corridor light was on a time switch.'

'And you were not hurt at all.'

'Only where you lay on top of me.'

'Oh I'm so sorry,' he smiled good naturedly, 'You used to

enjoy it.'

'Yes, I rather think I did.'

'A long time ago now.'

'I haven't forgotten.' I said.

'No, neither have I.'

'You said you were lucky.'

'Yes, it seems I received a bad flesh wound but at least it was only a flesh wound. They have bound me up and I should be able to leave hospital fairly soon. I do realise, you know, we could both have been killed so easily.'

'The thought had entered my mind. The world could have suffered a great loss.'

'Oh a great loss.'

We chatted on about inconsequential things, half teasing each other, half inquisitive. I asked him about his family and in particular his father.

'He was a good man,' said Charles, 'but he worked so hard, and attended so many committees that I didn't spend enough time with him, so didn't get to know him as much as we would have liked. Our mother ruled our house, my dad was someone we saw on Sundays and on holidays. I have some fine memories of him, playing with me on the beach and things like that but also some strange ones. I know one shouldn't judge someone for doing things which at the time they were done seemed acceptable, but looking back, he had some dangerous habits especially with young children around.'

'Dangerous habits.'

'Looked at from this distance in time yes. For example, he had an old Austin Seven Car, for technical reasons the starter motor never worked. To start the car, he would make sure it was parked at the top of the hill, then he would sit my sister and me in the back of the car, my mother in the front passenger seat, he would release the hand brake, keeping the driver's door open, the gear in neutral, and then would run with the car as fast as he could urging the car along by pushing on the steering wheel. At the last moment he would jump into the driver's seat put the car into gear and let the clutch out. What would have happened to us and the car if he had lost his footing is not worth thinking about. I am sure it never occurred to him how dangerous it was.'

'Yes I see what you mean. Why didn't the starter motor work?'

'It was broken,' he laughed.

'Oh very technical.' I could see Charles was getting tired, and after a little while I decided I had better leave.

On my way out of the hospital I bumped into Jeffrey Barrett again. He told me that he had just been to see the man who had ambushed us and knew him by the name of Kev.

'Short for Kevin?' I asked.

'Probably.'

'Do you know him.'

'I know I have seen him before.'

'Why did he want to kill you?'

'It is all to do with drugs.'

'Will he try again?'

'Given half a chance.'

'You are not such a good person to be around, Mr Barrett.'

'It goes with the territory,' he said and he walked off.

I went to call on Rosemary but she was still asleep, so I returned to the Bull and did some work: accounts, recruiting, advertising, pricing structure, stock levels. I suspect that all my staff would have had an easier time if I hadn't been there but I was pleased with my day, the Bull was doing well.

At 4 o'clock I went back to the Lister Hospital and went straight to Charles's ward only to find he was surrounded by friends and relatives. I crept away without being spotted. So far I had not even had a peck on the cheek or a term of endearment for well over a year so my status was still very questionable. My wanderings took me to Rosemary's ward, there she was, no nurse present, she was covered in tubes but conscious. I breezed in.

'Hello,' she said.

'Are you feeling better?'

'A bit, I am still worried, but not frightened. I can't understand why Kevin hasn't been to see me.'

'Kevin!'

'My son.'

'I had forgotten that your son was called Kevin. Does he live with you?'

'Oh yes, well most of the time; he often stays with friends so I don't see as much of him as I used to, that's only natural now that he's an adult but I was expecting him to visit me today.'

'What does he look like?'

'Here's a photograph of him, mind you it was taken a year or two ago now. Until about three years ago, he was a normal lad, then things changed and I am sure it was only because of drugs. Incidentally that conversation we had before my operation, forget it would you?'

'Yes but ..,'

'Just forget it, OK'

'Not really, you tell me you have murdered someone and I am just to forget it. Frankly I think you have got it wrong, Mr Barrett is a really nice person, he might even work for the police.'

'Lucy he is a bad man. I don't understand why nobody will listen to me, truly he is evil but as I say, best forget it, I will deal with it in my own way.'

'You said you would try to attack him again.'

'I think I know how I can prove that he has been trading drugs. You say you think he is a good man, I have worked out how I can prove he's not.'

'Are you going to tell me?'

'No, I don't want anyone to spoil my scheme. Have you ever thought he might be running with the hare and also with the hounds?'

'What are you trying to say?'

'That your idea of precious Mr Barrett is a long long way

from being correct. I haven't been able to work it out before but lying here, wait and see.'

'I haven't told you about last night yet, someone shot Charles.'

'Shot, you mean with a gun?'

'Oh yes, very much so, in the leg. I was with him, we were both shot at but he missed me.'

'Did they catch the man?'

'Yes but I don't know who he is.'

'But you thought it might be Kevin.'

'Well the man's name is Kev.'

'You have now seen his picture, does it look like him?'

'I have never seen him, so I have no idea.'

'My Kevin would never do that.'

'I'm sure he wouldn't, unless it was to get even with someone for the sake of his mother.'

'I can see you don't believe me on either count.'

'Either count?'

'That my Kevin didn't shoot at you and Charles, and that Barrett is evil.'

'It is a little difficult to accept.'

There seemed nothing else to say, so I left her bedside, she was a troubled lady.

I made my way back to Charles's ward to find him still surrounded by members of his family, they made room for me and I spent half an hour with them mainly listening to the problems of a middle aged lady, presumably his aunt, the problems were of a medical nature. At least Charles sent a smile in my direction every now and again.

There seemed little chance of seeing Charles alone that afternoon so after not too long I made my way out of the ward, waited for the lift by the window overlooking the green countryside of North Hertfordshire, and took the lift down to the third floor which is the floor giving access to the main exit. I walked along the wide corridor and into the foyer where coffee was being served and where the reception desk was situated, proposing to make my way to the car park.

A man, little more than a tramp, was asking the person behind the reception desk something in a much too loud voice. Like most of the people walking along the corridor, I gave him a wide berth not wanting to get involved, until I heard him mention Rosemary's name. I slowed my pace and walked closer to the man.

'I want to see Rosemary Parker, she is my mother,' he was saying.

'You can't go into the ward in that state,' said the receptionist.

I stopped, 'Are you Kevin?' I asked.

'Who want's to know?'

I wasn't over-keen to get involved, so shrugged and moved on. He followed me.

'Yes I'm Kevin.'

The receptionist had already turned to deal with someone else, relieved I think, of not having to argue further with this gentleman.

'What's your surname?'

'Parker.'

'And Rosemary is your mother?'

'Yes, and she is here somewhere, I need to see her.'

Although it seemed unlikely, this was indeed the missing Kevin, which meant that the man now held by the police, was not connected with Rosemary. I had firmly believed that the Kev and Kevin would be one and the same. I owed Rosemary an apology.

'Come with me,' I said, and headed for the lifts again. 'Until you are with her, do not say a word, otherwise the chances are you will be turfed out.'

'Mums the word,' he said giggling. 'Get it, mums the word.'

I led Kevin back to the wards, along the now too familiar journey into the lifts and along the corridors. I directed Kevin to the room where Rosemary lay and pushed him in, I stayed by the door, when Rosemary saw Kevin her face lit up, she beamed.

'Now do you believe me?' she said to me in triumph.

'About Kevin most certainly,' I said.

'And what about Jeffrey Barrett?'

I gave her a smile for an answer.

'I can prove it,' Rosemary said as I turned to go. 'I can prove Jeffrey Barrett is not what he says he is.'

I closed the door, bumping into Jeffrey Barrett as I did so, he was walking along the corridor outside Rosemary's room.

'What are you doing here?' I asked him.

'I noticed Kevin downstairs, and thought it might be worth following him for a minute or two,' said Jeffrey Barrett.

'And was it?'

'I rather think it was?' he said.

I walked out of the hospital again and into the car park, took the ticket off the windscreen and drove to Hitchin. I had no plans save to return that evening to see whether Charles would be allowed to go home. I had asked him to telephone me if he had any news. At the Bull, I went up to my room, coming over quite tired, I slipped my things off, lay on my bed, and in due course, fell asleep only waking at about 9.30 pm, far too late to for hospital visiting. I showered, dressed, went downstairs to the kitchens for some supper. Claude my chef was there, thinking about the following day's menus. He sorted me out some bits to eat, basically a cup of broccoli soup, a piece of steak, some mashed potatoes which he slipped into the frying pan with onions, herbs and mushrooms, adding a few peas and gravy to the warmed plate. He offered me an array of desserts all of which were tempting but I refused.

I chatted to Claude whilst eating his offerings which were delicious, a real treat, then went into the bar and helped out for a while. It being Saturday evening they were always glad of an extra hand or two, especially someone authorised to move cash around or ask clients very nicely to be a little less boisterous. Occasionally someone usually the worse for drink, would insist on seeing the manager and Martin was quite happy to pass onto me the duties of being troubleshooter. I served several rounds of drink, receiving for my efforts a £2 tip which I added to the collection the staff on duty that week shared, and spent the rest of the evening continuing the endless task of collecting up and washing glasses.

I had known all of the bar staff who were on duty that evening for many a long year and there was lots of friendly banter between us all. None of it rude, except to complain about the size of someone's behind when trying to squeeze past. The bar staff all called me Her Nibs, strangely this term of endearment, if that's what it was, had never spread to the rest of the hotel. Martin had always called me Lucy, everyone else, outside the bar staff called me Miss White, at least that's what they called me to my face. The particularly strange bit was that a member of the bar staff calling me Her Nibs in the bar area, would call me Miss White in the hotel area but perhaps that was how it should be.

I rang the bell for last orders, I always did if I was about, a sort of ritual, I then helped to stock up some of the shelves with mixers, put the cash into the hotel safe and said goodnight.

❧ CHAPTER 13 ❧

Sunday morning, I stretched and yawned and then made a cup of coffee and took a biscuit from the facilities provided in the hotel room. I was interested to see how the new facilities were faring. The kettle still looked new, the cup was china, not polystyrene and it was sparkling clean and unchipped, but we still had to use something called non dairy creamer instead of milk, so the coffee didn't have a wonderful taste. I telephoned Charles's ward but was just told that he was as well as could be expected. I think I was talking to a junior nurse who gave me the standard Sunday morning response.

Moving about the bedroom I caught sight of myself in the mirror, I swear that I was ageing by the day, without make up I didn't look my best. What to wear? Nothing too showy, in the end and after two false starts I opted for light green combat trousers with a camisole top printed with a design in Cambridge Blue. Skipping breakfast I walked out to my car, listening to the church bells as I went along.

When I was a teenager I had taken a course on bell ringing. It is very technical. Ringing a peal with seven bells is exceedingly complicated and takes years of practice to do properly, even learning how to start is difficult. First learn how to ring the bells up onto the balance, then the bell captain directs ringing rounds, treble down to tenor. That's just the warm up. The captain will call changes invented long ago, probably in the fifteenth century. They have been

218

perfected over the years, especially by an eighteenth century parish clerk called Fabien Steadman who invented method ringing. I found the whole thing very difficult indeed, just understanding it needed a computer brain, let alone carrying out the instructions; 'Four on two' might be called, I knew this meant bell number four follows two, so that five would follow three; that's the easy bit. The Bell Captain would move it along, calling 'Seven on one' and to change from one to the other the bell is left on the balance a shade longer, or shorter as required, really difficult. Then he would call a method such as Reverse Canterbury Pleasure, or Steadman triple. It's not easy, get it wrong, and it is so easy to break the stay, I nearly had a nervous breakdown every time I went.

I fished out my car keys from my shoulderbag reminding myself as I did so, that I really must sort the contents out, and opened the car door. I backed the car out into the hotel's main car park and drove the five miles to Lister Hospital. Although it was Sunday, car parking charges still applied, yet the car park was almost empty, as were the corridors and the lifts. I found Charles was sitting in the day room, washed, shaved, even dressed, looking both expectant and bored.

'Hello,' I said breezily, 'You look a different person, are you leaving this place today?'

'I wouldn't bet on it, there doesn't seem anyone around who can authorise my release. My it's good to see you. I've been sitting here for ages wishing I had something to read apart from these magazines.'

'I meant to pop in yesterday evening but fell asleep, sorry. I must have been very tired. Are you really mending?'

'I have to wear this strapping and can only move with a wheelchair except for the odd step, I should be much much better in a day or two. They just want me to take it easy for a little while to give things a chance to mend.'

'I could push you around, I'm good at pushing groceries around the supermarket in a trolley, it will be very similar I'm sure. I especially like the bit at the end when you push the wheelchair, sorry trolley as hard as you can so it connects up with the other trolleys squashing anything left in it.'

'I prefer the analogy of a passenger train where the engine, the unit in front, controls everything.'

'You don't look much like a railway engine, are you beginning to make funny noises?'

'Are you trying to get me moved up to the psychiatric ward?' said Charles.

'Would you be happy there?' I asked.

'I'd be much happier out of this place altogether. You look a bit frumpy this morning, I thought, to visit me, you might have made an effort.'

'I'll have you know that I spent 20 minutes in my room trying to work out what to wear. First you say I'm too smart and that you want me more frumpy, then you say I'm too frumpy. There's no pleasing some folk. From now on I shall consider you as a person with fickle taste and therefore not to be trusted as far as fashion is concerned.'

'OK let's analyse what you are wearing. You seem to have government surplus combat trousers on, no doubt bought from a charity shop.'

'Not quite, these are designer combat trousers made of thirty per cent polyester and seventy per cent cotton. They really are the height of fashion, and are carefully tailored.'

'Turn round,' said Charles. So I did, he peered at me. 'They came from government surplus stores.'

'I think you're bored and are spoiling for a fight.'

'I don't think I'm fit enough yet,' said Charles.

'Nor do I, that's why I will win, so I strongly advise you to mind your P's and Q's. I shall let you call me Miss White,' I said.

'Not Miss Whitewash.'

'Now if I press on your leg just here, you will probably have to stay in hospital for several more days just to ease the pain.'

'You never would.'

'Not a risk I would advise you to take.'

'I think you are a bitch.'

'I am,' I said.

'As long as we know where we stand, are you nasty with everyone or just with me.'

'Mainly with you. I don't think I am nasty to anyone else,' I said.

'So I do have a special place in your heart.'

'I expect it's the same place as I have in your heart.'

'Tell me true, have you just come to torment me this

morning or am I going to get pushed around?'

'Do you have a wheelchair?' I asked.

'Over there in the corner, by that set of crutches,' he said. I collected up the ghastly thing.

'Are these yours too?' I asked, referring to the crutches.

'Fraid so, but not to be used for several days yet.' I sat Charles in the wheelchair, whilst he did not complain, I could see this was going to be a trial for him.

'Let's go. Would you like the guided tour of the hospital, or the silent trip?'

'Very much the guided tour please, and you never know, there might be a tip in it for you.'

'You are in the wheelchair, and unless you are careful, you might be the one who gets tipped.'

'I didn't have you down as a bossy person,' said Charles.

'Shall we take the stairs?' I asked.

'To be honest, I think I would prefer the lift please, stairs can be a little bumpy in a wheelchair.'

We went to the ground floor where the shops were, but everything was still closed except the newspaper vendor. We made our purchases. We explored, going along corridors, through doors, up alleyways happily ignoring signs that forbade us to do so, ending up in the Accident and Emergency Department which at least had some life in it. We explored the empty canteen and then found ourselves on the route to the mortuary, so beat a hasty retreat. I paused not knowing where to go next.

'We could visit Kev,' I said.

'Kev. Who might he be?'

'Evidently he is the man who shot you.'

'Then lead on.'

Off we went up to the wards again but when we reached the side ward Kev was not there. The bed had been stripped, the room empty and bare, the bird had flown.

'Not surprising really,' I said, 'He was only concussed when I walloped him, he's probably enjoying breakfast in Hitchin Police Station at this very moment. I'll wheel you to see if Rosemary is awake yet.'

'We'd better go back to my ward first to see if I've been missed,' said Charles, 'It would be terrible if the consultant came to sign me off and I wasn't there.'

He had not been missed, indeed nobody seemed to be about at all. We retraced our steps to try to find Rosemary but her bed too had been stripped. The room was empty.

'She must have gone home,' said Charles.

'She was too poorly to go home,' I said, 'I expect she has been moved. I hope it wasn't to intensive care.'

We made enquiries, it took a little while to unearth anyone to ask.

'May I ask who are you?' said the nurse.

'Just friends.'

'I am really sorry to tell you that Rosemary died last night.'

'Oh no.'

'Unhappily yes. She had been very ill.'

'But I talked to her yesterday, she was recovering.'

'Patients do have relapses, it is very sad, she was a delightful lady. I am so sorry.'

It was a mournful journey back to Charles's ward, we were both engrossed in our own thoughts, one doesn't expect folk to die at such an early age, but of course it happens all of the time.

We made our way to the day room which was empty, I fetched some coffee, we spread the Sunday newspapers across the table and sat for a while, it was very peaceful. Poor Rosemary.

Eventually a registrar and a nurse came into the ward and took Charles off, he must have passed all the tests they had given him, and signed all the correct paperwork, for just a few moments later Charles returned in the wheelchair but under his own steam.

'Good news, I can go home.'

'That's wonderful, you look much brighter already.'

'They say that I must use the wheelchair for two more days, then crutches for a further two or three days, just to give this wound a chance to heal properly. Then everything should be back to normal. Incidentally, I do have an accommodation problem.'

'Is returning to your house out of the question?'

'Yes, I would never make it in a wheelchair, it would be impossible to manoeuvre up the stairs. What about your flat in London?'

'You would have the same problem, that only leaves the Bull.'

'I don't think I fancy living in a hotel.'

'It's only for a few days, and frankly, you don't have the choice.'

After much discussion he agreed the Bull seemed the only answer especially with the new access arrangements, constructed as part of the modernisation programme. We agreed that separate rooms would be best, not least to ensure Charles's leg mended speedily. I had to go into work the following day, Monday, but after that could probably operate from home as it were, making use of the Internet and the telephone. I drove Charles back to Hitchin loading the wheelchair and the crutches in the back of the car; the memory of him sitting in the wheelchair with a crutch under each arm but each crutch pointing forward like a two-handed jouster, is one that will stay with me.

Charles made good use of the new ramps at the Bull which allowed wheelchair access to all parts of the ground floor, and with the lifts, to the first and second floors of the building as well. I had not realised just how important that can be, instead of feeling behoven, he felt independent but it was early days, I left him in his room to sort himself out.

The day passed slowly and I felt at a loose end, a bit depressed, Charles had fallen into a deep sleep which was good for him but I would have loved to have talked with him. I didn't think it right to leave the Bull, so I started on some work. My next conference was in Birmingham, it was a comparatively easy one for me because the conference was a huge one, and a team of six of us were engaged on it. All the other operators were highly experienced and I was really only included in the team so that I would be able to get experience of organising on a very large scale indeed. Shorts have a book giving advice and instructions to operators, and each operator has a copy by her at all times. The book is called The Code. I thought an hour spent revising my knowledge of The Code especially in so far as it related to large-scale conferences might not go amiss, so I settled down in the lounge with a cup of tea and a note book. Most of what it said was obvious. The Code decreed never drink on duty, never be late, never accept presents, never be intimate with any client. There were other pieces of advice which were very sound. Keep a note of everyone's telephone number by you at all times. Try to get both a day time and an evening number. Have a contingency plan, suppose the venue burnt down, or the main speaker suffered from food poisoning.

I was still reading The Code and planning my part of the conference at 8 o'clock. I was to be responsible for everything before the conference actually started. That included parking, reception, registration, name tabs and making sure that everyone could grab a cup of tea or coffee and a biscuit in just a few seconds. Glancing at the clock I realised I had paid scant heed to Charles's plight all afternoon. I walked up to his room, not using the lift, as I had requested all members of staff not to use it and I was trying to lead by example. On the way up to Charles's room I overtook Gillian who was just coming on duty. We climbed the staircase together.

'Someone told me that your friend had died,' said Gillian, 'I am so sorry.'

'You probably knew her, Rosemary Parker, she used to work here.'

'Before my time I think. She was quite young wasn't she?'

'Thirty nine, or somewhere around there. We didn't see much of each other but she was a good sole and will be missed, especially by her son.'

'She died just after her operation?'

'Yes that's right,' I said. 'It seems she had a relapse, although when I last spoke to her, she seemed in fine fettle.'

'It happens.'

'The last thing she said to me was ... oh I am sure she was wrong.'

'Pardon.'

'It was just that she was accusing someone of wrong doings, and her death was very convenient to someone if she had been right; but I am sure she wasn't right, or am I.' I said.

'Are you saying that perhaps her death wasn't from natural causes?' said Gillian.

'No, I am sure it was, well fairly sure.'

'Tell me.'

'Just between the two of us,' I said.

'Of course,' said Gillian.

'My friend Rosemary, the lady who died, confessed to me that she had murdered Richard Jenkins, here in this hotel. She only meant to harm but it went too far. That's what she said anyway. By mistake she killed the wrong person. She said that someone called Jeffrey Barrett was very evil but I didn't believe her. The last thing she said to me was that she could prove Jeffrey Barrett was running with the hares and hunting with the hounds or words to that effect implying that on the one hand he was trying to catch drug dealers, whilst at the same time he was a drug dealer himself. I didn't believe Rosemary but as it so happens Jeffrey Barrett overheard her talking to me. Next day she is dead. Now I am sure that there is nothing in her allegation but ...'

'But you would like to be even surer.'

'I think there should be a full post mortem.'

'Very well, I will arrange it.'

'Can anyone just arrange it?'

'I'm not just anyone,' said Gillian.

'No of course not but eh, tell me, how can you arrange it.'

'You forget who I work for.'

'You work for me,' I said.

'I do indeed, but I meant my day time work.'

'I think you said you work for a firm of solicitors.'

'That's right. My boss is a solicitor, he is also the local Coroner,' said Gillian.

'I don't really know what the Coroner does.'

'It's a very old official appointment, going way back. Coroners hold courts when people die in unexplained circumstances, so that such deaths are all open and above board. Sometimes they sit with a jury, they decide other things as well, like treasure trove,' Gillian stopped walking, she had reached her first room.

'You have lost me.'

'A Coroner can order that a post mortem be carried out.'

'And will he do that for me?'

'I'm his secretary, I do all of the paperwork. I will simply prepare the appropriate forms and he will sign them, he always does. If there is any query over someone's death it is right and proper for the Coroner to be informed. Naturally I would not be able to stop a post mortem being performed but ordering one is almost automatic if there are doubts. You will have your post mortem.'

I left Gillian to tend to her work and I walked down to Charles's room. He was watching television when I walked in.

'You're awake.'

'Yes, have been for ages, in fact I thought I had been forgotten.'

'So sorry, I didn't want to disturb you, then got engrossed. How do you feel?'

'Sore and hungry,'

'Would you like me to bring a tray up to you?'

'I would rather have a change of scenery. Let's go to your

dining room.'

So we did. In fact Charles was in good form, we chatted about such inconsequential matters, as whether pink is a proper colour, or simply a shade of red. If its a shade of red, is green a shade of blue and what about dusty pink, or salmon pink. We turned it into a grand argument which was an irrelevance, it was such a fun evening.

During our meal Martin bought two bottles of wine for us to try.

'A bottle for each of us Martin?'

'Not necessarily. You wanted to try the Cotes-du-Rhone 1993 and the 1995 and here they both are.'

He poured half a glass of each into wine glasses for us both.

'Which is which?' I asked.

'Can you tell?' asked Martin. 'That's the whole question?'

Both Charles and I sipped from each of the glasses, the one really did taste much better than the other. After conferring we both agreed.

'We both like this by far the better.'

'Of course you do, I'll leave you the bottle and take this other rubbish away,' and he was gone.

Charles became serious.

'I have a problem next week,' he said.

'You can stay at the Bull, I have already reserved you a room, there is no problem at all.'

'It's not accommodation that is worrying me, it's my job. How do I look after all of those horses teeth if I am in a wheel chair?'

'Yes, a problem,' I agreed.

'You could help me.'

'I couldn't, I can't become an equine dentist over night.' I said.

'No, of course you can't.'

'What did you mean then?'

'If you were willing to help, I could get through. Do you have to work in London next week?' Charles asked.

'I have to go in tomorrow but I could work from here for the rest of the week, at a pinch.'

'I can't do anything until I am out of a wheelchair, that should be on Tuesday. After that they say I will need the two crutches for about three days. If I could get the support from the side of my van and ask you to fetch and carry for me so the pressure is off my legs, I could continue working.'

'I'll help you if I can, go through it again. What would I have to do?'

'You are good with horses. I've seen you, you have an affinity with them. I would ask you to fetch the horse to me, and to hold him. I would ask you to insert the steel jaws into his mouth, and strap them up. I can make a chart of the teeth sitting on the van's wing. With your support I can use my rasp, I can diagnose anything that is wrong. If an urgent extraction is called for, I will have to bring in a colleague.

After any work needed is completed, you can use the syringe to clean the horses mouth out and put him back in his stable.'

'Do we need to. If it's the money..'

'It's not just the money, it is far more than that, I don't want to lose my customers to my competitors. I have spent a long time building up my round and it is very easy indeed to lose it if one cannot provide a service. Most owners of horses, quite rightly, get very upset if their mount has toothache, often they are impossible to ride.'

'Will I be able to support you enough.'

'If I lean against the van you will. The muscle power required for my job comes from the shoulders, the van is the only solid thing which we know will be available at each of the stables, so we must use that. Will you try for me?'

'Of course I will, between us we will cope. Meanwhile do you want some pudding?'

'No, not really thank you. Charles began to get romantic again, he was delightful and complimented me on my eyes, my complexion, said how pretty I looked. He had had to sit in his wheelchair throughout our meal and after some coffee, I wheeled him out into the night air. The stars were set in a sky of velvet, there was the slightest of breezes, it was a lovely night.

'Let's go for a drive,' said Charles.

'OK,' I said. 'My car is over there, parked behind that Peugeot.'

'With not inconsiderable effort I pushed Charles in his

wheelchair over to where my car was parked, then hoisted him into the passenger seat, abandoned the chair and drove off. The roof was down, we were both really happy, at least I was very happy and he certainly seemed to be. We drove to Chicksands Wood on the road towards Bedford and there parked off the road, away from the world.

'I did miss you so very much,' said Charles.

'I was lonely and empty without you darling.'

'How did we have such a stupid misunderstanding.'

'My fault I am afraid.'

'I shouldn't have got cross.'

'Where do we go from here?'

'Do we have to decide now,' I said.

'I need to know whether we are together.'

'I am certainly together with you.'

Charles kissed me really tenderly. He twisted to reach my lips but it was not a good idea, he yelled out in pain.

'It's getting worse,' I said.

'No, just a bit too much activity in the wrong direction.'

I started the car's engine and drove back to the Bull, retrieved the wheelchair from its parking place, helped Charles into it, and pushed him into the lift and up to his room.

'It is a myth, you know, that people in wheelchairs don't need affection,' said Charles.

'I'd better see what I can do.'

I opened the bedroom door, he could more or less cope

then. I went away, to give him some privacy, returning after about ten minutes ready to be romantic and affectionate but he was already fast asleep.

I stroked his hair, and kissed his cheek, but he did not stir. Quietly I shut his door and returned to my room. I put some things in a small case, walked downstairs, explained to Martin that I was spending the night in my flat in Islington, jumped into my car and drove off into the night.

❧ *CHAPTER 14* ❧

My flat in Islington was on the first floor of a large Victorian detached property. Once, no doubt, the home of a fairly wealthy family with servants galore. Long since the servants had gone and the property had been divided up into flats, one on the basement, another on the ground floor, a further flat on the first floor, which was my flat and the top floor flat. Each flat had two bedrooms, mine were quite large but some of the others were not so fortunate, a sitting room, kitchen and bathroom. One of my bedrooms and the sitting room had been divided out of what must have been a truly enormous reception room of the old house. There was a good deal of plaster work, especially on the ceiling, some walls were very thick indeed, others lathe and plaster. The only drawback to the arrangement of the flats as they were at that time, was that one had to go through the sitting room to get to the second bedroom, but it did not cause many problems except when I was entertaining and my flat mate Peter was in bed and wanted to go to the bathroom. Peter was a really delightful person, friendly, artistic, thoughtful and gay. Proudly gay.

On my unlocking our front door, I found him in the sitting room watching a Big Brother repeat on television. He turned the television off immediately he saw me.

'I didn't really mean to watch it,' he said.

'Hello Peter, everyone says that about Big Brother. You

235

watch what you want to watch.'

'How did the conference go?' he asked me.

'Quite a success actually from all points of view, thank you for asking but there is real news,' I said. 'Yesterday evening, I was shot at and worse, my boyfriend was hit. Fortunately a glancing blow, all very dramatic.'

Peter is the world's greatest gossip. He pumped me for more and more details, I told him I felt grimy was desperate for a bath but he was not deterred, he simply sat on the loo seat whilst I bathed. I have never been comfortable sharing a bathroom with someone who was not a lover but tried to look upon the experience as if in a nudist colony, rather than a sexual encounter. Peter certainly viewed it that way.

I put out my clothes for the morning, a light red trouser suit with pink shirt, I needed to be noticed, our office was not the place to hide one's light under a bushel. I shared a coffee with Peter and, as it was then well past midnight, I turned in.

Arriving at my office the following morning, having journeyed down to the Angel then along the old City Road into Moorgate, I found my name had been placed on the wall-paper chart and that I had already been allocated another conference to organise. Business for Shorts obviously was booming. This was a one-day conference, so no accommodation problems, seven hundred delegates. These one-day conferences were the bread and butter work of Shorts, each of us organised two or three a year. They were not as complicated as a longer conference because as the hotel or conference centre tended to look after car parking, tea breaks and lunch. It was our job to recommend the venue, deal with numbers, speakers, provide badges and check loudspeaker systems, projectors and of course we dealt with any complaints. I took a really careful note of the client's requirements, e-mail addresses and telephone numbers which might be relevant. I then looked up suitable venues on the huge office computer, for Shorts kept a record of every venue, good or bad, that they had ever used for any function, with full data relating to that venue. Indeed it was one of our first jobs after completing a conference, to record the details of the venue we had used and fill in a questionnaire of how the conference had gone by answering on a computer a set of fifty questions. The task was not an arduous one, we just had to fill in, against each question, a number between one and ten. One meant very good, ten meant very bad. I had to complete such a questionnaire for the Bull, trying to be as objective as I could. So I gave my new bedrooms nine out of ten, but the facilities within the hotel only four as there wasn't a swimming pool or gym, the food received ten. Once the Bull was on the record it would be flagged up every time one of my colleagues wanted a venue for under fifty people.

I chatted for a while with some of the headquarters staff, they always had the latest news. Who had left the company, who had been promoted, who was in trouble, it is always interesting going back to the office, I feel in the centre of things, I get my faced noticed. I joined a group of colleagues

I knew vaguely and had a bite to eat with them, then drove straight back to Hitchin to find Charles sitting up in the lounge reading a whodunit. I walked in and looked round for the wheelchair but it was not in evidence.

'It's gone,' he said reading my thoughts.

'Should it have gone?'

'I don't like the crutches,' he said, 'but I hated that wheelchair. You'll have to be patient with me, I am very slow.'

'Did you get to hospital?' I asked.

'No, just to my doctors to get the nurse to change the dressing. It seems everything is fine but I must take it easy, but then they are bound to say that. All being well I can have the stitches out next week. Do sit down, come and join me for a cup of tea.' said Charles.

'Yes I will, that would be lovely, I'll go and get it straight away.'

'Lucy sit down,' he said, so I did. Charles rang a small bell that I hadn't noticed and very promptly Gloria came in.

'Hello Lucy, Charles, how can I help you?'

'Would you kindly bring Lucy a cup of tea, Gloria and perhaps a sandwich?'

'Of course I will,' said Gloria, and walked away.

'She fancies you,' I said.

'Of course she does,' said Charles, modesty obviously not being his strong point. 'How has your day been?'

'I didn't get much real work done, except to log on my last conference and to take down details of the next one allocated to me. I had lunch with some colleagues who I now know a bit better and came home.'

'Nobody time keeps up there, you don't have to work 9-5?'

'It isn't that sort of job.'

We chatted on, and later Gloria brought in a fresh pot of tea, milk, cups and a selection of sandwiches and cakes. I think it was the first time I had been properly waited on in the Bull's lounge. The sandwiches were fine but the cakes were fantastic, they were tiny versions of every type of cake you could think of. We had miniature chocolate eclairs, tiny jam doughnuts, miniature millefeuille - about fifteen different sorts - they were lovely, I had never seen them before. I think I ate twelve.

After tea, Charles wanted to go for a drive, in my absence he had made me a second driver on his van insurance, so when the last sandwich had been shared between us and the last cake argued over we oh so slowly walked over to the car park to where Charles had abandoned his van a few days earlier. The van had not improved in smell or looks since I had last sat in it all those months ago, in fact it smelt worse if anything and was still very untidy. I commented about this and Charles assured me that it had been pressure washed inside and out only a month or six weeks ago but that as soon as it was done, the smell seemed to return. I helped Charles in, torn between assisting too much and not helping enough. Once properly installed, I went to the driver's side, slipped into the seat and started the engine.

'What a pong.' I said.

'Sorry.' said Charles.

'It reminds me of a girl friend of mine, who lived with a chap for ages, then he threw her out of his house, even though she had been paying him board and keep. She got her own back by hiding some bits of raw fish everywhere she could think of around the house. She put them behind the fridge, behind the cooker, under the sink, even inside some brass curtain rails. The smell in that house was just like it is in this van, are you sure you don't know her?'

'I will get the car cleaned out, I promise.'

'Where to then governor?' I asked.

'Back to my house in Stevenage please,' he said, 'I need to get some more clothes and things, then off to a pub.'

'There are lots to choose from.'

'Let's go to one of the pubs in Offley.'

Our plans for the early evening were made. I stayed in the car whilst Charles went into his house which was more of a maisonette, for various bits and pieces he needed, I had proposed to go with him to help him but he was adamant that I mustn't.

'You've got something to hide,' I said.

'Of course,' he said.

'Why can't I share your secret?'

'Well, because.'

'That's what they say to children.'

'Mmm, yes it is, I won't be long,' and with that, very

slowly, on crutches, Charles walked off.

He was gone a very long time, almost an hour, and when he came back he was empty handed.

'I couldn't carry it,' he said, 'It's outside the door at the top of the steps, would you get it for me please?' So I did.

I drove to Offley and parked under a copse of trees at the edge of the car park. The view from the pub garden was truly amazing, breathtaking. One could see for miles. In the bar, we met some of Charles's friends, in the right quarters, he was very well known. Naturally we had to go through our story for about the hundredth time, we had a drink or two with them. As I was driving, mine was a drink, non alcoholic and as Charles wasn't driving, his was the two, in fact he probably had a few more than two beers, but who was counting. We spent a convivial evening during which I got to know another side of Charles and in fact that is how the following week passed, not in the pub but me getting to know him rather better. We spent all day every day working alongside each other, I learnt of his beliefs, his fears, his dreams.

Each day we donned our wellies, jeans and rugby shirts worn over a tee shirt, and drove to a set of stables, sometimes remote, sometimes in the centre of a village. Charles would introduce me, we were always offered tea or coffee and given a biscuit, everyone was sympathetic to his plight. We would drive the van as near to the horse as possible, I would fetch the horse, open its mouth with the steel contraption. Charles would examine the teeth, write out his chart, then carry out the necessary remedial work. Once finished I would rinse the horses mouth out and the job would be done. Most of the owners or grooms had known Charles for many years but not as a close acquaintance, only as someone who visits twice yearly. It was all very amiable.

Travelling between stables Charles would chatter happily about his job, his van, the horses and the people he met. He told me that he gave the people silly names, to fit in with their perceived characters. He had a Mrs Always Smiling, a Mr Dirty Clothes and a Mrs No Cup of Tea, also Mrs Fancyable. I had to be very careful what I said to each of them, they would have been horrified if they had known; if I had called Mrs Clare de Winchurch, "Mrs Stuck up".

'Do you have a friendly name for me?' I asked him.

'Several.'

'What are they?'

'I never tell. I can tell you I made a limerick up about you.'

'Was it rude?'

'Yes, a bit.'

'What rhymes with Lucy, Lucy, moosey, cousey, I give up.'

'Try rhyming White.'

'That's easier, light, plight, kite, height.'

'Yes it's a grand name to use. You have hardly touched the surface. Might rhymes with White, as in "Lucy White's a lass who might",' said Charles.

'Charming,' I said.

'That's not the limerick's first line.'

Chapter 14

'So what is?'

'I'm not telling, so drive on please, Miss Lucy White, a lass who might, go far if ....'

I kissed him, to shut him up, and started the engine. He held my hand and squeezed it for a moment before I moved the gear lever and edged the car forward. He stroked my wrist as I drove, running two fingers up and down the lower part of my arm.

By Wednesday morning Charles was feeling much better, his leg still hurt if he twisted it, or rubbed something against it but otherwise the worst seemed to be over. So much in fact that by Wednesday evening he was obviously feeling frisky. As we had not had any sort of sexual interaction since we had split up all those months ago, I thought perhaps it time that this was remedied. All the usual sexual positions would cause him great pain, I would have to be inventive. I was sure if I put my mind to it, I could give him a little bit of fun without him ending up in Lister Hospital with torn stitches.

Personally I hate wallpaper music but we did have a speaker system in the function room and the reception area. Most of the music was classical, reflecting Martin's personal taste, I flicked through the tapes stacked at the side of the stereo unit and chose Ravel's Balero. Dressed in black underwear, a slip, long black skirt and a deep red blouse with many a button up the front I entered Charles's room clutching my tape player. He greeted me with a smile, I started the music and slowly danced and disrobed, getting more frenzied in line with the music. When the music stopped I was standing in my knickers. I gathered up everything and made as if to leave.

'Is that it?' he asked.

'Well, yes it is.'

'You still have half your clothes on.'

'Is there a problem here?'

'I thought you were giving me a strip-tease?'

'Did it work?'

'Might have done.'

'Well there we are then.'

'That's like being given a Ferrari but finding it has a wheel off and you can't go anywhere.'

'That would be frustrating.'

'It is frustrating.'

I looked at him, he was sitting on his bed, fully clothed, leaning against the headboard.

'Aren't strip-teases meant to be frustrating,' I asked lying down on the bed on my tummy, my feet overhanging the end, my face was almost level with his waist. Slowly I undid his zip, he rose to the occasion, I played, nibbled and licked him.

'Let me see your bum,' he said.

'Say please.'

'Please.'

I put my lips around him and at the same time somehow managed to pull down my knickers so my rear was exposed. I tickled him until he came to a climax, it was worth it, he saved my life just a little while later.

Thursday came, and everything changed.

Thursday morning started bright, with just a bit of a breeze. We breakfasted as usual over coffee, toast and boiled eggs, with all of the physical work I was doing I allowed myself a slightly more substantial breakfast. Dressed as true workmen we drove out to a well kept farm near Welwyn.

'Morning Mr Ames,' said Charles, 'Let's be having a look at them then.'

'Who's this your new colleague, Charles and why are you on crutches?'

'This is Lucy White, Lucy this is Mr Ames.'

'Come to learn the tricks of the trade have you? It's very simple, I don't know why we bother to call Charles out sometimes. Really anyone could do it yet I'm sorry your hurt, do we get a discount?'

'A discount Mr Ames, now why should you want a discount?'

'You're obviously not wholly up to the job being injured as you are. My dear,' he said turning to me. 'Julian is in that stable, would you get him out please?'

I went over to the stable expecting to see a groom but no, Julian was a magnificent Trakehner stallion. These warm blooded horses originated in Germany and have been favourites of top show jumpers for many years. This horse, Julian of all names, behaved a little restively to start with but soon calmed down. I put a halter on him and lead the great beast out into the yard.

'Come along then,' called out Mr Ames, 'Over here, let's have a look at you.'

I brought the horse over hoping Mr Ames wanted to look over the horse, rather than me. As it was, I think I was the main attraction, he had seen Julian's rump many a time. I bent over to pick up the steel jaws, feeling the man's eyes on me, put the jaws in Julian's mouth and adjusted them properly. Charles did his stuff, producing a chart, then his rasp, I did the syringing.

We had our cup of tea, said our goodbyes and then moved onto another stable where, this time, seven horses were waiting for us. I realised that if one owner needed the services of an equine dentist, often he or she would ask round all of the other horse owners in his vicinity if they also could make use of him, helping to reduce the overall cost. They all knew each other very well. It turned a visit to the equine dentist into a social occasion with several riders hacking over to the one set of stables, waiting there for the equine dentist to attend to their horses teeth, and then hack back.

Fortunately Charles's wound appeared to have improved beyond measure, the stitches still had to come out and he was still using a crutch but could take several steps unaided. I think he only used the crutch now because I was with him and he knew I would nag him if he didn't. He still used the van to lean against but that was more of a protective measure; he wasn't quite sure how much pressure he could put on his body without causing more damage, better to play safe. Lunch we had in a pub in Tewin, we looked in another set of stables in the afternoon and then made our way home to the Bull.

Charles did not seem at all tired, we showered together, he wearing a large black plastic bag over his wound to keep it dry. When I tried to give him a cuddle, he winced as soon as I touched him. It seems our love making would have to wait. I dressed for the evening in light brown cord trousers, long sleeve top and a dusty red jacket. It had been a good day again, we each had a glass of what we fancied before supper, and then chatted over our day whilst eating braised guinea fowl with figs and oranges, I think my chef put it on the menu especially for us which was very sweet of him. In the evening, in the saloon bar, we challenged each other to a game of cribbage, and played until about 8 o'clock when Gillian came over to find me. She had just come on duty.

'There you are,' she said, 'I've been looking for you. Hello Charles, are you recovering?'

'Hello Gillian,' we both said together.

'I've received the results of your post mortem, well, not yours exactly, if you follow me; you were correct, Rosemary Parker died of a massive overdose of heroin. There's to be a full police investigation although there's nothing to show that it wasn't self administered.'

'Self administered!'

'Many people, unhappily, end their lives by their own

hand, sometimes deliberately, often by mistake. I'm not investigating things, you asked me to arrange for a full post mortem to take place and this I have done. Incidentally the police are bound to want to interview you again, as you were, in effect, the initiating party.'

'Gillian I am really grateful to you. A heroin overdose, I know it wasn't self administered.'

'The pathological report is quite clear, it was an overdose. The Coroner doesn't go into details of how or why, I think he was quite pleased to clear the hospital of the cause of the death, statistics being what they are. By the by, I am not meant to have told you, certainly not yet, don't let on that you know will you, the police only had their copy this afternoon.'

'Thanks so much Gillian. I am surprised they did it so quickly.'

'Yes, often post mortems take a week or more, it always depends. I must get on,' she said, and she left Charles and me to think over what she had told us. We tried to come to terms with what Gillian had said, discounting Rosemary's wish to end her own life, which we did. As far as we knew, she only told me and Kevin, that she had worked out how to prove Jeffrey Barrett was working under different colours but certainly Jeffrey Barrett had overheard what she had said to me. It was going to be embarrassing if Jeffrey Barrett was present when I was interviewed by the police, he was almost certain to be there.

We were mulling these thoughts over, the two of us, when

Gloria came into the bar, evidently she had been looking for me.

'Ah there you two are,' she said, 'There is a message for you Lucy. Someone wants a word.'

'Right just coming,' I said, and followed her out of the bar, and into the reception area.

'Evidently its confidential, he would like to talk to you outside, he's waiting by his car.'

'Who is it?' I asked.

'Sorry didn't catch the name.'

I walked out of the rear door of the Bull, into the car park, and had the shock of my life. I was grabbed from behind and a pad with something impregnated into it, held against my mouth and nose. I passed out.

I woke up, sitting in the manager's office, feeling awful, very nauseous. I did not know how I got there, or what time had passed. I just sat, recovering my senses, all alone. I didn't feel well enough to get up or call out. I just sat, slowly recovering, breathing hard. I could still feel the hand on my face. After what seemed to be an age, I lifted the telephone and told Gloria that I didn't feel very well and would she kindly get me a glass of water. She came into the office within a few moments.

'You look really dreadful.' she said.

'I feel really dreadful,' I said.

'No I mean it.'

'Oh believe me, I mean it too, someone has just attacked

249

me.'

'You what, here drink some water, you poor thing. What on earth happened?'

'Really I don't know, I passed out. Tell me what you remember.'

'Let me think. Someone came into reception and said they needed a quiet word urgently. I found you in the bar, told you someone wanted to talk to you, you went to the car park, a few minutes later Charles followed, I did not see anything else until you called me in here.'

'So Charles is still out there alone with some brute,' I said in some alarm.

'I'll go and see,' said Gloria.

'Be careful, take someone with you, he might still be out there.'

After a few minutes she came back to report that there was nobody in the car park at all. Most worrying of all, Charles, it seems had vanished. Slowly I recovered, the sickness went, just leaving me with a headache which was more persistent. I lay down for a while, fell asleep and when I woke up, which was much later, Charles had returned. It was very late.

'Are you awake?' he whispered.

'Yes, what happened?'

'I have just been on a bit of a wild goose chase.'

'Yes, but what happened, I was attacked.'

'I know you were, I gave chase.'

'On crutches?'

'I drove my van.'

'I think we should call the police.'

'No, really I wouldn't.'

'But he might do it again.'

'Did you see him, could you describe him?'

'No.'

'Then what would you say to the police. It is bound to affect the reputation of the Bull. Bad publicity.'

Much troubled, I turned over and slept.

Friday morning greeted me with a clear head and greeted Charles with a very lazy feeling, all he wanted to do was to lie in. I got him up eventually, we had a quick, very late breakfast and I drove to the first appointment. Charles fell asleep on the way.

'Anyone would think you had been up all night,' I said.

'It certainly feels like it,' said Charles.

'Don't keep yawning, you will start me off.'

'Sorry,' he said, and yawned again.

'The day itself was really a re-run of the day before, different horses, different stables, otherwise identical, save for a very sleepy Charles. Every time we drove anywhere, he slept. He slept over lunch and as soon as we returned to the hotel, he went to bed. I woke him up for supper and then he went to bed again. I asked him whether he thought he was ill but he just said it was a reaction setting in and not to worry.

During the week I had been able to do precious little of my own work, so I spent Friday evening making up for this. I had expected the police to call to arrange an interview and sure enough the summons came through, asking me to go to Hitchin Police Station to be interviewed by D.C.I. Blake. We agreed 11 o'clock the next day, Saturday.

With all the sleep he had had, I thought Charles would be as bright as a button on Saturday morning but he was worse if anything. He stayed in bed until long past breakfast and was still snoozing when I left to visit D.C.I. Plod. Charles usually worked on Saturday mornings but evidently not this Saturday; I didn't begrudge him his rest, I just worried about him, it seemed to me to be something of a relapse.

At the police station D.C.I. Blake interviewed me accompanied by another attractive young policewoman. I was so pleased to see that Jeffrey Barrett was not present. Naturally he asked me why I had suggested that a post mortem would be appropriate in respect of Rosemary's death.

'She died so suddenly, yet seemed to be doing so well.'

'Even so, I understand that she had had a series of major operations, there must be more to it than that.'

'Yes there was. Just before she died, when she was in hospital, Rosemary, said to me that Jeffrey Barrett was, as she put it, running with the hares and hunting with the hounds. She accused him of both being a drug dealer and attached to the police, trying to catch drug dealers. Rosemary added that she had worked out a way to prove what she believed was true, was true. Jeffrey Barrett must have overheard her say that to me. I didn't believe her, I thought she was wrong. Now I'm not so sure, anyway, next day she was dead.'

'That's a very serious allegation you are making.'

'No, no, I make no allegation at all. You ask me a question, I answer it. All I am saying is that I know Jeffrey Barrett overheard Rosemary's remarks and next day she died. I must admit that I thought Mr Barrett would be present today and I was rather dreading saying this in front of him.'

There was a long silence.

'I don't see why I shouldn't tell you but please don't speak to anyone else about it. We have lost contact with Jeffrey Barrett just for the moment.'

'Ah!' I said.

'It doesn't mean anything,' said D.C.I. Blake.

'I think it does and so do you.'

'He might have been hurt by someone else.'

'Or he might have done a runner.'

'I don't think so. We are still inclined to think that Rosemary's overdose was self inflicted, she was in very low spirits after her operation. Her son Kevin was a known drug user, very unreliable. He could easily have furnished Rosemary with enough heroin for her to end her life. Jeffrey Barrett is often out of touch with us for a few days, it is the nature of his work. I mention it only to indicate that we are taking what you have said seriously and will put those points to Mr Barrett as soon as he surfaces again. In the meantime I would like to go over things with you.

You certainly seem to be in the middle of things again. This is the second suspicious death in which you have been involved, in as many years.'

'That's because they are linked.'

'Linked, the death of Richard Jenkins at the Bull and the death of Rosemary at the hospital are linked?'

'Oh yes, just before her last operation, Rosemary admitted to me that she had killed Richard Jenkins.'

'What!'

'Before she died, after her second operation but before her third operation she told me that she had killed Jenkins but that if I told anyone else, she would immediately deny it. She poisoned him but meant to poison Jeffrey Barrett as was suspected.'

'Why didn't you tell me earlier?'

'I wasn't going to have you cross question her when she was facing a life or death operation. I was going to drop you a hint when she had recovered a little. I did tell Jeffrey Barrett.'

It took nearly three hours of questioning before D.C.I. Blake was satisfied that I had told him all that I knew, then he allowed me to return to my sleeping beauty at the Bull, for sure enough, Charles was gently snoozing when I walked into his room. I was beginning to wonder if he was ill, but again he insisted that it was just a reaction to the shooting, which I suppose it was. We all react in different ways to crisis in our lives.

Sunday again. I listened to the bells of St Mary's whilst

having breakfast on my own. I was in bed and asleep before 10 o'clock these nights and woke up early as a consequence. Charles had now been sleepy for several days and nights, I couldn't see how he could possibly manage his job for the following week but he said he would be able to cope. I told him three times that I had to return to London to earn an honest crust. His reply was that few people in London earn an honest crust, I told him he was cynical. In the end I telephoned everyone I could think of and eventually agreed terms with a friend of a friend to act as driver and gofer for Charles for the week. Later I heard that she was stunning, wonderful company and very rich, but I did not know it at the time and as the saying goes, what the mind does not know about, the heart does not grieve over.

Although I had to work in London the following week, it was easy for me to commute from Hitchin, so that is what I did. I rose at 6 o'clock, caught the train and returned home to have supper with Charles. We even managed a cuddle or two. On Wednesday of that week, Charles had his stitches out and had fully recovered his wakefulness, I don't think the two were related.

It was on Friday that startling news hit the papers.

'Local man arrested for murder,' read the headlines in very large print indeed. Underneath the headline it read:

"At Stevenage Magistrates Court Jeffrey Barrett was charged with the murder of Rosemary Parker and was remanded in custody for two weeks." It then gave details of the post mortem findings, details of which had already been leaked to me by Gillian.

The news raised more questions than it answered but there was nowhere I could go to get any answers. I telephoned D.C.I. Blake but he was very tight lipped. It was all quite mystifying. Eleven months or so later, I read that Jeffrey Barrett had been convicted at St Albans Crown Court of the murder of Rosemary Parker and he was given a term of life imprisonment. Normally that would have been the end of the story, indeed it was the end of the story for many months. Then one day, whilst Charles and I were walking along the beach at East Runton in Norfolk, with our shoes and socks in our hands and the surf tickling our toes, unexpectedly he told me what had really happened.

❧ CHAPTER 15 ❦

It was a lovely day but the sea, the North sea, was exceedingly cold and there was a wind that made us glad of our jumpers. The locals said the wind came direct from the Russian Urals, it certainly felt like it. Nevertheless we had taken our shoes and socks off, at least Charles had taken his shoes and socks off, I seldom wore socks, and we were walking along the sand hand in hand at the edge of the tide, allowing the freezing surf to trickle over our toes.

We had parked off the road near the centre of East Runton which, at it's heart, seemed not to have changed for centuries, with its flint walls all very quaint but not in a chocolate box sense. This was a working village, fishing and farming, life there had been hard. We had walked down to the sea through a gap in the cliff, passed old tractors which had been pulling fishing boats out of the water for decades and then passed the boats themselves.

Half way along the beach towards Cromer, there's a pill box left over from the second world war. For decades it had lain forgotten, half buried in the sands. There we stopped and rested for a few moments hiding against its thick walls out of the wind and it was there that Charles told me the rest of the story as he knew it. Many months had passed since Jeffrey Barrett's trial, the events leading up to it had been dusted and put away.

Charles and I had been chatting about work and friends

and people we had known. Naturally the Bull was mentioned.

'You must be quite pleased with the way your hotel has prospered over recent years,' said Charles.

'Quietly contented, yes. We seem to be on an even keel, making a fair return. I am quite proud of the place.'

'The murder at the Bull didn't do you too much harm then?'

'No, not noticeably.'

'I never did tell you the rest of the story, did I?'

'The rest of the story, the rest of what story, what do you mean?' I asked.

'Promise, don't tell a soul.'

'I won't tell a soul, promise.'

'That evening,' said Charles, 'Soon after we heard that the post mortem report showed Rosemary had died from an overdose of heroin, do you remember?'

'Can I forget.'

'You left the bar to talk to someone, Gloria gave you the message.'

'Yes, just after we had talked with Gillian.'

'I followed you out into reception, in fact I followed you all the way out into the car park.'

'Yes I know Gloria saw you.'

'I saw you being attacked. I had to hit the attacker on the head to stop him hurting you.'

'Why didn't you tell me before, who was it, do I know

him?' I asked.

'All in good time. I hit him on the head with an empty coke bottle, it was the only thing I could lay my hands on. He went out like a light.' said Charles.

'You are very strong.'

'I picked you up, made sure that you were still breathing and somehow carried you into the manager's office.'

'I wasn't that heavy.'

'It wasn't your weight that was the problem, it was my injured leg, I daren't put too much strain on my stitches. Anyway I sat you down in the chair in the manager's office, checked you over a bit, then thought I had better do something with the attacker. When I went back out into the car park ...'

'Let me guess, he was gone.'

'Not a bit of it. He was still lying on the ground, where he had fallen. I didn't fancy being charged with assaulting him, I wanted to know why he had attacked you, so I bundled him into my van and drove off.'

'But your leg, I mean, how did you carry him?'

I didn't need to carry him, I reversed the van to where he lay and eased him into the back. I drove to a set of stables I knew were deserted of people but not of horses, the horses there knew me and I knew the combination number of the pad locks. It was a set of stables where I had horse-sat some six months previously.'

'You were lucky he didn't wake up.'

'Oh he did, I walloped him again.'

'I see.'

'When we reached the stables he was still unconscious, I backed up the van as far as I could and pushed him onto the ground. I took off all of his clothing including his shoes and socks, and put my boiler suit on him, that old one I kept in the back of the van.'

'Why?'

'I didn't want anyone to be able to trace where he'd been.'

'I still don't understand.'

'It will become clear. I then used my duct tape to ...'

'Duct tape ...?'

'It's two inch wide black tape, really strong. Everyone has it.'

'I don't think I do.'

'I used my duct tape to bind his legs together and his arms behind his back, I gagged him using binder twine and threw him into the middle of a pile of hay bales. I then went back to the Bull to see how you were.'

'Who was it?'

'It was Jeffrey Barrett, but I didn't know who it was at the time.'

'Good heavens.'

'Quite. Well to continue my story, I waited until the hotel was asleep, then made my way back to the stables. Barrett was very cross with me, except he didn't know who I was.'

'He was still there.'

'He was certainly still there. He was furious, I dare not let him see who I was, I had taken with me one of your chef's aprons and I put it over his head. I cut off his gag and he started to scream. It didn't matter as we were miles from anywhere and he was in the middle of a hay rick stacked indoors in a large barn, no sound could escape. Nevertheless I didn't want him to keep screaming so I stopped him.'

'How?'

'Do you really want to know?'

'Yes.'

'I put a finger over each of his eyes and pressed down telling him that every time he screamed I would press harder. He stopped instantly. I made him call me sir. I asked him questions but he would not give me proper answers.'

'So what did you do?'

'It was getting late, I gagged him again, left him where he was and returned to the Bull and went to bed.'

'How long for?'

'I went to bed for the rest of the night.'

'You know that's not what I meant.'

'I left him trussed up until the following night but we, you and I, did drive past during the day time to make quite sure that all was quiet, there were no cars around. You weren't aware why we drove that way.'

'So he was lying there in the barn the whole time we were out during that day tending to the horses teeth.'

'Yes he was.'

'What happened the next night?'

'I borrowed your cassette recording machine from the office at the Bull. I went to bed as usual and again got up in the dead of night and drove out to the farm.

I found him very dejected. I cut an eye hole in your apron and dragged him into one of the empty stables, it was pitch black. I wasn't quite sure how to make him talk, as I am not much of a torturer but I thought the horses might help me. I brought a huge stallion 17 hands or more it was, into the stable and shone the light from my torch onto the horse. Barrett became nervous, he didn't like horses, funny how some men don't, women too of course. Barrett was frightened and desperate for a drink. I pushed his head into the water trough four or five times, I didn't want him to drown.'

'What did you do?'

'I shoved him onto the floor, so he was lying very close to the stallion's hooves. I asked him to tell me what had happened. Unhappily he didn't reply.'

'So what did you do?'

'I decided that I should frighten him rather than hurt him. I pulled him on top of the horse so he was lying down along the line of the horse's back, with his arms and legs dangling down either side of the horses flank. His head was at the tail end. I tied a piece of rope to each of Barrett's four limbs and then tied the ends of the rope together under the horses belly. Barrett could go nowhere, unless the horse went too. I put a numnah under the ropes to stop the stallion's coat being damaged.'

'How did you get Barrett to talk?'

'He couldn't stop shaking but he swore and swore at me. I gave Barrett a very gentle push just enough to disturb his equilibrium, just enough so that he slid down the horses side and hung under the horse by his limbs my knots in the ropes now being on top of the horse's back. Barrett's head hung awkwardly so that after a short period his neck muscles started to ache, I left him there for about half an hour.

I then turned the torch on so that Barrett could see the predicament he was in. I walked the horse around and said the horse would be trotting soon unless he talked, he hesitated, he was thinking about the options and then the horse peed on him. As you know when horses pee they really pee, unhappily Barrett's face was not far enough away for him to avoid being splashed. A bit more than splashed actually, Barrett had had enough what with being tired, hungry, thirsty, and frightened. He talked.'

'What did he say?'

'He spilt the beans as they say. All I wanted to know was why he had attacked you. I said to him, "Tell me everything", and once he started talking it all gushed out, but I stopped him and made him talk slowly and methodically into the tape machine. Remember at this time, I still didn't know who he was, or of his connection with Rosemary.

I made him give his name and address then confirm that he

made the statement of his own free will.'

'But he didn't, you forced him to make it. It would not be admissible as evidence.'

'Well he said on the tape that he made it of his own free will and that's what counted. I didn't want to put words into his mouth, so only said "go on" occasionally. I had to turn the tape off every time I spoke.

He went on to say that he had joined the security services and was seconded to the police to liaise on the drugs question and to try to catch some of the big fish. It meant infiltrating the drug rings and to make it more realistic, he was authorised to trade in drugs in a small way, otherwise his cover would soon be blown.

He realised that he could make a great deal of money very quickly. His cover with the police gave him absolute security from arrest, all he had to do was to trade in drugs just to a larger extent than was authorised and pocketed the difference. Soon it became very large scale indeed. He started importing drugs, he learnt the names of the co-drug runners and give those names to the police to help him keep his cover. It also got rid of a competitor.'

'A dangerous game.'

'But a lucrative one, he became very rich. It seems he thought Rosemary had been trying to stop him, she was his loose cannon. He had overheard her say to me that she could now prove he was double dealing so he killed her with a heroin overdose. That should have been an end to his problems but you insisted on a post mortem, an autopsy. He found out about it only that afternoon and was desperate to stop you talking to D.C.I. Plod, if you had, everything would have come out into the open.'

'This must have taken a long time, the travelling, the planning and carrying it all out, no wonder you were so tired during the day.'

'I need my beauty sleep.'

'You can say that again.'

'Sometimes you can be horrid. I really don't know why I love you. Anyway, getting back to Barrett, I made him tell me on the tape where all his money was, then when I thought he had told me everything I let him down, secured his arms with duct tape and pushed him back to his nest amongst the hay and then bound his feet together. I gave him a cheese sandwich and a drink of water, I didn't want him to pass out on me - that would have queered my pitch - and gagged him again. During these long sessions, the stallion was wonderfully patient, just standing munching at a net of hay I had given him.'

'Let's walk on, I'm getting a bit chilly,' I said.

We strolled on along the beach towards Cromer.

'The next night I made him repeat everything he had told me, this time with a fresh tape in the machine. I secured him under the stallion again, I made him go through everything and said that if there was any change in the previous night's story, it would mean to me that one of them was untrue, I told him that I wouldn't like that at all. I was particularly keen to make sure that he recorded all of his bank accounts, especially the foreign ones and all of his contacts. Those he couldn't remember he gave details as to where the information could be found. Then I cut him down so he fell between the stallion's hooves, I dragged him off.'

'So that's the end of the tale.'

'Yes; almost. He was already thirsty, and extremely hungry, I gave him some salty crisps to eat and orange juice laced heavily with vodka, he became drunk, very drunk. He consumed in the end almost a whole bottle of vodka. I knocked him out, he would have a grandad of a headache, what with all the drink and being hit; I undressed him, putting his own clothes back on him, I hated doing that: I shoved him into the back of my van and took him to another set of stables some twenty miles away where they only kept ponies. You and me, we had visited those stables earlier in the day, I needed to check that they were both suitable and deserted at night. I let out one of the ponies to graze in the meadow and pushed Barrett into the empty stable and gave him more vodka and poured a full bottle of whisky over him. I locked the stable door, drove away and anonymously called the police.'

'But the police would see your tyre marks, they would know it was you.'

'If I had ever been questioned and I never have been, I would readily have agreed that I had been there. It was my job to do so.'

'Barrett would say that you had kidnapped him, then tortured him making him record the statement.'

'He never saw me. I always spoke to him in very short phrases, very very high in tone. I reasoned that he would tell the police he had been kept in the middle of the hay stack, but he wouldn't have known it was a different hay stack. There would have been no trace of him in the hay where he was found to substantiate his story. He would have complained that he was suspended under a very large horse but there were no large horses about. I posted copies of the tapes off to the local Member of Parliament, the local newspaper, the local police and the county police. I didn't know who else might be in the scam with him so needed to spread my information as widely as possible. All that was then left to do was to get both the inside and the outside of my van steam cleaned just in case I was connected with anything and throw away the old boilersuit Barrett had worn. My hope was that when the police arrived at the stables in answer to my telephone call, they would find a man much the worse for drink, talking gibberish. Nothing he said would link up and they would not take his accusations seriously.

Next time I saw the stallion, I gave him a mint as a thank you. In fact I have a roll of mints on me now. Would you like one?' asked Charles.

'As a thank you.' I enquired.

'It's certainly payment of some kind, probably more than

you usually get.'

'Why do I hate you sometimes.'

'Part of my charm.'

'Oh, is that what it is. Never would I have guessed.'

Walking along the beach we had reached the base of the huge columns supporting the pier and stretching way above our heads. Charles suggested walking its length so we retraced our steps making our way first onto the promenade and then onto the pier itself. Hand in hand we walked along the boards, stepping around the fishermen each of whom seemed to have five or six lines stretching far out into the rough sea. We didn't see anyone catch anything, but then I never have. At the end of the pier, we found space for ourselves and leaned over the parapet watching the sea roar towards the columns and then retreat, we braced ourselves against the Force 6 wind or perhaps it was Force 5.

There, with nature in front of us, wild and exciting, Charles proposed marriage to me.

❧ CHAPTER 16 ❧

But I said no. I did not want to marry Charles, at least not yet.

Living permanently together would have presented severe problems for both of us. Charles is content with his equine practice in North Hertfordshire, he is still carefree and charming. He is loved by both the horses he looks after and by the ladies holding the end of the halter; he still lives in his bachelor apartment and I still haven't been allowed to cross the threshold. Charles for all of his delightful qualities, is untidy: he simply does not see the mess he creates.

Me! I still work for Shorts, in exactly the same job as before. I have refused promotion as it would immediately lead to a desk bound job organising, enthusing and controlling people or selling Shorts to the world; I would much rather be out actually running the show, I think I am good at it. I know I am organised, I am tidy, I don't mind the checking and rechecking.

No doubt someday, perhaps when we want to start a family, the bridge will have to be crossed and compromises made. I will have to give up my Islington pied a terre, Charles will have to quit his tiny house, together we may buy an abode more suitable to bring up children but until then, there is little need.

We see each other nearly every week. Some weekends Charles takes the train into town where we go to the theatre, catch a film, or eat in a fancy restaurant with friends. Some weekends we stay at the Bull together, I park my immaculate Porsche next to his white van, the same white van as he has always had, just a little more tatty. Often one or both of us have a weekend away, not infrequently for Charles, on a rugby tour especially in the winter. I have discovered a love for France, not so much her wine but her way of life. The area around the channel ports is not France at her best, so usually we fly to a provincial airport, hire a car and stay in a one-star, or less, hotel. I am trying to improve my French.

And so the extraordinary sequence of events concludes. Unfortunately it left two people dead and a man in prison for many a long year. Fortunately it left the Bull prospering and me, with the dearest of friends.

Murder at the Bull Hotel
the Novel by Claire Hall

I wish to order a copy of Murder at the Bull Hotel with a BLUE/YELLOW* spine and enclose my cheque for £4.99 (inc. p&p £1.00).

*Please specify whether you wish to receive Murder at the Bull Hotel with a BLUE SPINE = a delightfully **sexy** love story with a touch of humour, encased in a 'who dun it?' or a YELLOW SPINE = a delightful love story with a touch of humour encased in a 'who dun it?'.

If you do not specify a yellow spine book will be dispatched.

Please send cheque payable to:
Abbeyhill Publishing Ltd.
Abbeyhill, Broadway, Letchworth, Herts.

Name: ....

Address: ....

....

.... Post Code: ....